KOOLAIDS

KOOLAIDS

THE ART OF WAR

RABIH ALAMEDDINE

PICADOR USA

NEW YORK

Picador® is a U.S. registered trademark and is used by St. Martin's Press under license from Pan Books Limited.

For information on Picador USA Reading Group Guides, as well as ordering, please contact the Trade Marketing department at St. Martin's Press.
Phone: 1-800-221-7945 extension 763
Fax: 212-677-7456
E-mail: trademarketing@stmartins.com

The art on the title page shows *Hélas #185*, a painting by Rabih Alameddine (courtesy Harriet Green Gallery, London); from a photograph by Ira Schrank, 6th Street Studios.

Book design by Gretchen Achilles

Library of Congress Cataloging-in-Publication Data

Alameddine, Rabih.
    Koolaids: the art of war / Rabih Alameddine.
        p. cm.
    ISBN 0-312-18693-2 (hc)
    ISBN 0-312-20658-5 (pbk)
    1. Lebanon—History—Civil War, 1975– —Fiction. 2. AIDS
(Disease)—Patients—Lebanon—Fiction. 3. Gay men—Lebanon
—Fiction. I. Title.
PS3551.L215K6 1998
813'.54—dc21   98-4879
                                                                                          CIP

First Picador USA Paperback Edition: July 1999

10 9 8 7 6 5 4 3 2 1

TO MY FATHER,

MAY HE FORGIVE ME ONCE MORE

The author is grateful for permission to reprint the following copyrighted materials:

"Israel Spurs Lebanon Exodus," © The Associated Press, 14 April 1996; reprinted by permission.

"Why Beirut and Not Damascus?" by Arthur K. Vogel, *Tages-Anzeiger*, reprinted by permission of the author and *Tages-Anzeiger*.

"Yet pray even while. . . ," translation by Lionel Salter of *"Bete aber auch dabei"* © 1997; reprinted by permission of the translator.

"Parliamentary Elections" and "What Is a Lebanese Anyway?" by Joseph L. Boohaker; reprinted by permission of the author.

"Lebanon First," © *The Jerusalem Post*, 13 August 1996; reprinted with the consent of *The Jerusalem Post*.

ACKNOWLEDGMENTS

This book is a work of fiction. It is not a biography. Lebanon is a small community, and I anticipate readers who will imagine characters herein to correspond to real persons. They do not. Everything is a creation of my twisted imagination.

I appropriated the words and ideas of many authors in this book. In most instances, these authors spoke directly to the narrators. There are a couple of sentences in the book, however, which I simply stole from Nabokov, Coover, or Borges. I need to mention Jean Said Makdisi's autobiographical book, *Beirut Fragments*, which inspired a number of vignettes.

I would like to acknowledge the help of a number of people for this book. William Zimmerman read the book numerous times. His editorial work is inestimable. My sister read the book and gave her approval. I would not have published the book without it.

I would also like to thank Richard Labonté for believing in me. He introduced my manuscript to a number of agents. My agent, Norman Laurila, worked hard on my behalf. I would also like to thank Michael Denneny, my editor, for taking a chance with my manuscript. He opened my eyes to how a great editor works.

Anne Marie Crichton once told me to write about my dreams. When I sat down to write, they were the only thing I could write about. I thank her. Carolyn Chiappelli taught a naïve engineering student how to read Shakespeare. Carlo Togni and Maya de la Rosa Cohen inspired me. Ed Huntress showed me what good writing was about, and Rick Wallach gave me the confidence I needed. I would like to thank Erica Sorensen for asking to be mentioned in my book. Last, but not least, I would like to thank my family, my parents and my sisters, for enduring an errant nonconformist all these years.

I wonder if being sane means
disregarding the chaos that is life,
pretending only an infinitesimal segment of it is reality.

Death comes in many shapes and sizes, but it always comes. No one escapes the little tag on the big toe.

The four horsemen approach.

The rider on the red horse says, "This good and faithful servant is ready. He knoweth war."

The rider on the black horse says, "This good and faithful servant is ready. He knoweth plague."

The rider on the pale horse says, "This good and faithful servant is ready. He knoweth death."

The rider on the white horse says, "Fuck this good and faithful servant. He is a non-Christian homosexual, for God's sake. You brought me all the way out here for a fucking fag, a heathen. I didn't die for this dingbat's sins."

The irascible rider on the white horse leads the other three lemmings away.

The hospital bed hurts my back.

———

Time. Time is what I need right now. I can't think straight anymore. I should not have said that. I try never saying the word *straight*. Let's say I can't concentrate. That describes my predicament accurately. I can't speak English anymore either. Really. I can't think in English. It's back to my roots. I now think and dream only in Arabic. I haven't done that for the longest time.

1

James was here the other day. Or was it today? I can't think straight. Time gets very confusing.

James says something to me. I reply. He has that look of utter confusion. He doesn't understand a word I say. I switch to English. It's really easy for me to switch between two languages. I actually can communicate clearly in three. French is my second language. English is my third. Most Lebanese can speak three languages. I can really speak only two. French has been completely forgotten. I have not dreamed in French since I was a boy. I spoke English when I was a boy. It actually was the first language I spoke. I had a nanny who spoke only English. She was from Liberia. She was black. So is James.

James sits on the chair in front of my bed. I lie down quite a bit these days. He always asks how I am feeling. Great, James, I am feeling great. I am not dying. He always implies that I am. James sits on the chair in front of my bed. James looks tired. He is slouching. His socks don't match. It isn't as if they don't match in the classic sense. That is, they do not match anything he is wearing. My father says a man's socks must first match his tie. If that doesn't work, they must match the shirt; followed by the jacket, if it is different from the pants. Pants should be the last match. If none of that works, one is supposed to wear black socks. But if you ask me, one should go out and buy socks which match. James is wearing white tube socks, and that simply does not work since he is wearing nothing else which is white. He is slipping. I tell him, but he doesn't understand me. I must have said it in French and he doesn't speak French. Most Americans speak nothing other than English. Hold on a second. I am an American and I speak French, so that statement does not describe my predicament accurately. Actually, French has been completely forgotten and that describes my predicament more accurately.

James sits on the chair in front of my bed. He looks tired. At thirty-nine, he no longer looks as young as he did. Neither does my father. There was a time when James was handsome. Or was he just nice-looking? I can't remember that far. I ask him why he comes so often to visit me. His mouth drops. I guess he understood what I said. I must have said it in English. James looks so cute when he is shocked. His eyes get so wide.

———

I open the door for Kurt. "Hi there," he says cheerfully. I grunt acknowledgment and head back to my chair. He comes into the living room, where Scott and I are sitting. Scott puts his book down to receive a kiss from his latest boyfriend.

"What are you reading?" Kurt asks, picking up the book. He sits on the arm of the chair and tousles Scott's hair. "*Spanking the Maid*? That's a provocative title. What's it about?"

"Spanking the maid, of course," Scott replies. He picks up another book. There are no less than eight books on the table next to him.

"I wish I could read as much as you do," Kurt says. "This is such a short book. It's not a book. It's a short story."

"It's a novel, or whatever Coover wants to call it. A book's length is irrelevant."

I wonder how long this relationship is going to last. I continue reading the paper, trying to ignore both of them.

"I guess you're right," Kurt adds. "Still, I probably would prefer books that are more substantial than this. Something which takes time to develop."

Four weeks tops.

"Here, let me read you this." Scott picks up a Calvino book. "You might find it interesting:

Long novels written today are perhaps a contradiction: the dimension of time has been shattered, we cannot love or think except in fragments of time each of which goes off along its own trajectory and immediately disappears. We can discover the continuity of time only in the novels of the period when time no longer stopped and did not yet seem to have exploded, a period that lasted no more than a hundred years.

"Do you follow this?"

"Not really," Kurt says. "Are you ready to go to the movie?"

"Sure."

Two weeks. Not more than two weeks.

———

James took his friend's hand and kissed it. "I come to see you because you're my best friend," James said.
"You should go out more often," he said and burst out laughing.
"I know. I know."
"I'm not your best friend, James," he said. "I never was. I was Scott's best friend. We had him in common."
"You're my friend, Mo," James said. "You are my friend."

4

March 20th, 1976
Dear Diary,

This day is without a doubt the worst day of my life. The shelling was getting closer to our apartment. My husband thought it was okay to go to work today. No problem, he said. They won't be fighting here, he said. The children were underfoot all morning. The maid was having another Egyptian anxiety attack. She was no help. When a loud shell exploded, she let out a bloodcurdling scream which made Joumana cry. I wanted to slap her, but didn't risk it. Then it happened.

We heard the whistle long before it hit. It must have been only a few seconds, but it seemed eternal. The only thing I remember about those seconds was the look in Samir's eyes. He heard it. I heard it. We looked at each other. The shell exploded on a floor somewhere below us. The whole building shook. Every pane of glass in the apartment exploded. The children screamed. I screamed. The maid did an Egyptian pirouette and fainted. I yelled at the kids to get moving. We were going down to the shelter. I was proud of how calm I was. I had been expecting this for some time, but one never knows how one will behave until it actually happens. Samir slapped the maid, bless his little soul, and shoved her out the door. We ran down the stairs, which luckily were undamaged.

God in all his mercy decided to send my husband home just in time. We met him going down the stairs. We took him down with us to the makeshift shelter in the building's underground garage.

We arrived at the same time as the Sanyuras. Labiba Sanyura was in her nightgown. How embarrassing for her, I thought. She did not even have time to put something on. Although, with her weight, she should not walk around the house in a nightgown. The children were all excited. They tried to find out the news from each other. My husband asked if anybody knew which floor was hit. Someone said the shell had hit the fourth floor. My first thought was how lucky we were to be higher up. This made up for all the times I cursed our luck having to use the stairs to go up eight flights when the electricity was out. As if we all had the same thought at the same exact instant, we all looked around to see if the Habayebs were down here. They were not. I started praying they were not at home. I realized it was not very likely. My eyes started tearing.

Najwa Habayeb is my friend.

My husband, bless him, said someone should go up and check on them. Basil Rawda screamed, "Are you crazy?" My husband said, "If they are up there, they would need our help." Rawda, who is a very unpleasant man, said, "Then you go up. If you want to orphan your children, you go up." My husband got a hard look in his eyes, which I knew so well, and said he was going up. I was so proud of him. Najib Hafez said he would accompany him.

I told my husband I was coming along. I had to check on Najwa. He convinced me I was acting silly. We could not risk both our lives. They left and stayed up there for fifteen minutes. I started getting hysterical. Rawda told me my husband was crazy. I told him he was an asshole. That shocked both of us. He never said another word for the entire day. My children were distracted, but I kept waiting. The shells kept falling and falling. I felt my control slipping.

When my husband came into the garage carrying Najwa, her face covered in blood, I lost it. I screamed. The children screamed. Mr. Hafez, who followed my husband, was carrying Marwa, Najwa's four-year-old daughter. Everybody stared at them in disbelief. I got myself under control and ran to help my husband put her down. He told us Najwa's husband and three boys were dead. Killed by the explosion. Najwa was hit by two pieces of shrapnel. One was lodged in her stomach and the other seemed to have cut her forehead. Marwa, who was in the middle of everything, was completely untouched. We had no bedding or pillows down in the garage. I sat down and placed Najwa's head on my lap. My husband covered her with his jacket. We had to wait a long time before we were able to take her to the hospital. They all left me with her and started talking among themselves.

I don't recall much of what happened for the twelve hours before we were able to drive her to the hospital. All I remember is Marwa never left our side and she never cried. I also remember talking to Najwa constantly even though she was unconscious. I remember singing her favorite song to her, *"Tal'a Min Beit Abuha,"* which translates into "She's Leaving Her Father's House."

———

Scott died in 1990. They never really figured out what finally killed him. You know how some people die and it seems just right? They are at peace. They have a glow about them in their last days. They say the wisest things. Scott wasn't one of those.

———

A time unknown. A life unborn.

My life has become nothing but regret. When the nurse told me I was HIV positive, I wanted to scream. Hold on a minute. Hold on. I haven't even begun to live my life. I thought I had more time.

After a childhood of complete and utter confusion, I started grasping who I was when I turned fourteen. It was not a single event which precipitated a change. It was gradual. My fourteenth year, 1974, was the happiest year of my life. I had finally adjusted to living in Lebanon. The war started in 1975. When I was told I was to be sent out of the country, I wanted to scream. Hold on a minute. Hold on. I haven't even begun to live my life. I thought I had more time.

———

THE WORST PAINTER OF ALL TIME

When Ben Baxter noticed his first KS lesion, he went on disability. Having worked as a corporate benefits consultant, he had set himself up well. He was covered, and would be able to live on disability for the rest of his life, albeit a shorter one now. Nevertheless, he handled his early retirement, as he called it, with gusto.

Ben's lover was an accountant who loved to paint. He had gone to art school, and spent a lot of his free time copying the masters, both traditional and modern. Art being a part of his life, Ben decided he too could be a painter. Now that he was living the life of leisure, he could concentrate on being an artist. With the help of his lover, he got set up with materials as well as a gorgeous, large easel.

Now, one has to know that Ben was crazy, or maybe I should just say funny. After all, he was a New Yorker, and had a master's degree in psychology from Columbia. Come to think of it, I take it back, he was crazy. We got along very well. We were, for whatever reason, the closest of friends, even though I was unable to stop making fun of him. It may have been because both of us were East Coast queers living in San Francisco.

At the time, some things in my life were changing. I had seen an exhibit of my friend Mohammad's work at a downtown gallery, and my whole view of art changed. For the first time, I started entertaining the idea that maybe I could paint. I walked into Ben's house for a dinner party. Ben was strategically placed before his canvas with a brush in his hand. "I just have to add some touches," he said, and kept adding touches until all the dinner guests came in. That was Ben, not just a painter, but a drama queen too. The painting was a copy. Since his lover copied all the masters, Ben was following in his footsteps. Except Ben was not copying any of the masters, he was copying a bad painter who painted naked Asian boys. The original paintings were really bad: no depth, no understanding of color, and composition from hell. Ben's copies were worse, and throughout his "career," he never got better.

I learned a lot from Ben's painting. Technically, it was the first time I saw anybody do a grid to copy a painting. It was an epiphany. I had never thought of myself as being able to paint because my drawing skills were atrocious. Watching the grid, I realized maybe I did not have natural ability, but I sure could do that. More important, I watched Ben. Painting became a panacea for all that ailed him. His spirits were lifted. I was so impressed, I asked Ben to help me start painting.

Ben was very helpful, but he was very confused by how I started to paint. My first paintings were like nothing he had ever seen and he made sure to tell me so. Whereas Ben was studying naked Asian boys, I was studying color. These paintings were formless, nothing more than color explosions. At that point I had very little interest in representation, while he thought naked Asian boys were what art was about. Let me elaborate a bit about Ben's paintings. The originals he copied were very flat. They looked like color by numbers. Draw in a sky and fill it with paint, draw in the eye and fill it with paint. Ben's were even worse. I once asked him if he thought the sky was all one color, cerulean blue. He had no idea what I was talking about. Whether it was sunset, sunrise, cloudy day, or sunny day, Ben's skies were always cerulean blue.

Ben and I got our first show together. It was a nonjuried show by the local gay bulletin board service to which we both belonged. I did not feel I was ready. I had been painting for about five months, but the show was done because of the notes which I uploaded to the BBS when I started painting. I could not back out. Ben, on the other hand, was ecstatic. People were about to see his genius! He entered one of his naked Asian boys and a copy his lover made of Léger's *La Lecture*. He proudly told me nobody would be able to figure the Léger was a Léger copy since *La Lecture* had not been seen in the US since 1945. How can one explain that anybody can tell a Léger painting because of the style? It was then I realized he was simply artistically blind. Couldn't see worth shit. It is said that Skinner taught pigeons to tell the difference between a Monet and a Matisse. Those pigeons could tell more about painting than Ben.

Ben continued painting and produced one horrible painting after another. He thought they were all masterpieces. He gave them to friends. They never knew what to do with them. They hid them in closets and brought them out when he came to visit. He kept on painting. He kept on painting until he really couldn't see worth shit due to CMV retinitis.

Ben died this morning at 5:19 A.M. The world lost a bad painter and a great soul. I miss him already.

———

I always thought if Beethoven could do it, so could I. The truth is I am not Beethoven. Hell, I am barely a John Tesh. When I started losing my eyesight, I could not paint anymore. I could not force myself. My dealer said she would be able to sell out a show if I came out with some new paintings. I could not. I destroyed all my paintings, even the 60 by 80s I kept for myself. My studio is deserted. If I could not see my paintings anymore, no one else would.

I heard some collector sold one of my paintings to the Museum of Modern Art for five times what he paid for it three years ago. They must think I am dead or something.

———

Georges was my introduction to bisexuality. He was bisexual. I wasn't. He porked both my cousin and me. That made him a bisexual. It also made him my hero.

A big scandal erupted when it was found out he had deflowered my cousin. My stupid cousin arrived home with a smile on her face and blood on her panties. Her father threatened to blow off Georges's head. She claimed he forced her. He claimed otherwise. They were both fourteen. Her father could not shoot Georges since he was so young. Many of my uncle's friends suggested he would feel much better if he shot Georges anyway. My uncle settled on being miserable for the rest of his daughter's life. My cousin, who was a fairly attractive girl, ended up dying a spinster at an early age. Her father was able to be happy after her funeral.

Cervantes told me history is the mother of truth. Borges told me historical truth is not what took place; it is what we think took place.

So Billy Shakespeare was queer.
Ronnie was the greatest president in history, right up there on Mount Rushmore.
AIDS is mankind's greatest plague.
Israel only kills terrorists.
America never bombed Lebanon.
Jesus was straight. Judas and he were just friends.
Roseanne's parents molested her as an infant.
Menachem Begin and Yasser Arafat deserved their Nobels.
And Gaetan Dugas started the AIDS epidemic.

———

I met Scott in 1980. We were both twenty. I saw him across the dance floor at the Stud. I knew who I was going home with that night. Scott was my type to a tee. Pug-nosed, baby-faced, blond, with a cute butt was my kind of boy. I walked all the way across the space and cornered him. Convincing him to come back home with me was a piece of cake. All I had to do was mention I was a painter. He had a thing for artists, he said. I had a thing for cute blond things. He said he loved my accent. I said I loved his butt. Off to my studio in North Beach we went.

We never consummated our desires. We arrived at my studio. I turned the light on. He walked over to the painting I had finished that day. He stood in front of it entranced. At first I was flattered. After the first five minutes I started getting horny. I stood behind him contemplating my painting and started rubbing my crotch on his behind. The scene was turning me on. Fucking the cute butt of a boy admiring a painting of mine was my idea of heaven. Scott then started to speak and I lost my erection. He started telling me about my life, my dreams, my fears. He started telling me about my mother, about my father. He told me about the war which tore my life apart. He related what he saw in the painting. It was the first 60 by 80.

We spent that night in bed talking. We never fucked, ever. He meant everything to me. That first night he started calling me *Habibi,* which means "my lover" in my native tongue, a cognomen which nobody ever questioned, not even his future lovers. He never used my real name, or any of the numerous Americanized nicknames I picked up along the way. I had always assumed he found it difficult to pronounce. I was wrong. His last words before he took his last breath were, "I love you, Mohammad." An impeccable pronunciation.

———

We live in a neighborhood called Galerie Semaan. It is named after the furniture store which designates the edge of the neighborhood. The area will become famous years later because of the fierce battles that occurred there, but for now it is simply my neighborhood. It is on the southeastern side of Beirut, about a mile from the beach. It is right on the edge of Beirut, after which you have the mountains and the various suburbs. The neighborhood proper consists of about ten buildings, most of which have the six floors allowed by zoning in the area. It is bounded by the road to Chouifat and the South on one side, and an orange grove on another. On the west side, there is something called the New Road, which is neither new nor a road, but a wide gravel path beyond which are slums where Palestinians and some Shiites live.

The northern side is dominated by the Beirut-to-Damascus road. Although we live in a flat section of Beirut, the Beirut-to-Damascus road starts a steep incline right at the edge of our neighborhood.

For us kids, the boundaries are very important. We really cannot leave our neighborhood. We cannot cross into the orange grove because the guardian shoots trespassers, particularly if they are kids. I see him sometimes with his shotgun. He hunts birds that come into the grove. Hunting is everybody's favorite pastime. My dad tells me the guardian is harmless. None of us kids wants to risk it. We also do not go past the New Road. We don't mix with the people who live there. One day our neighborhood boys crossed over to play soccer on an empty lot there. Once we started playing, all the slum boys came out and wanted to play against us. We played them. We won, of course, since we were much better. When the game was over, the slum boys beat us up. We never cross that line again.

———

Amalgam.

I am back at the Berkeley campus. I am passing by the Arts building. Bullets fly overhead. A soldier shouts at me to get out of the sniper fire. He leads me into a warehouse. We enter an office together. I find the soldier extremely masculine. I am terrified of him. I am in awe of his sexuality. I ask him if I can suck his cock. He shrugs. I kneel in front of him as he leans back on the desk. I unbutton his fly. I take out his cock. I am surprised at its size and rigidity. I start sucking. As I do, the soldier begins to transform. He develops breasts. His hair grows longer and fairer. I am still sucking his cock as she becomes a gorgeous woman. I still find her exciting. I do not want to ever stop sucking her cock. I can feel her getting bored. She takes her cock from my mouth, stuffs it back into her panties, and straightens her dress. She exits the building as I run after her, offering her money to let me suck her cock. She walks on the arms of a handsome man. She looks back at me and smiles. She keeps walking away. We are back in Beirut.

———

The call of death is a call of love. Death can be sweet if we answer it in the affirmative, if we accept it as one of the great eternal forms of life and transformation.

Hermann Hesse wrote that. He was full of Jungian crap. I told him so myself. I told him what I thought of his friend, Jung, as well.

———

Georges calls my name. I see him at the entrance of our building's garage. Today some people shot at other people. Everybody got scared and stayed indoors. It is calm now, so Georges is downstairs. He calls me again. I go flying down the stairs to see what he wants. He says he has something to show me. Am I interested? Sure, I say. I would do anything he wants. He is my hero.

He takes me down into the garage. He leads me to a dark, secluded corner. It is dark, damp, and putrid. He asks me if I want to see his cock. I say sure. Only if I drop my pants, he says. My pants come flying off. He shows me his cock. It is beautiful. You can touch it, he says. I do. You're a natural, he says. I am aglow. Turn around and bend over, he says. I do as I am told. I feel his hands massaging my ass. I feel a wet finger penetrate me. It feels uncomfortable. I like it. You're a natural, he keeps saying. I am proud. I feel him press something bigger against my ass. I know what it is. I am not stupid. I try to help him, but it gets too painful. He is all the way in. It hurts a lot, but I like it. You're a natural, he keeps saying. He keeps pumping until he gets rigid and shouts all of a sudden. At the same instant, the sound of gunfire erupts again, so I can't distinguish what he is shouting.

He pulls his pants up. He looks at me and smiles. He says we'll do that again tomorrow. I say, sure. We both run up home to find out what is happening. My dad is on the roof, trying to figure where they are fighting. I run up to join him. I am so excited. I hang over the safety railing and look in the direction of the fighting. I stand on the lowest railing hoping to see better. My dad says we should go back down to the house because he sees some men with their faces covered running towards the Beirut-to-Damascus road. Just as he says that, some other men a little farther off start firing in their direction. My dad starts moving towards the roof's exit. I am still excited. I still stare at the fighting. I see this incredible thing. It is coming at me at an incredible speed, but I do see it. The bullet comes at me pretty fast and it hits the metal railing right in front of my crotch. The bullet calls my name. I go flying down the stairs to get home.

———

September 5th, 1988
Dear Diary,

Today is without doubt the worst day of my life. Samir told me he has the AIDS virus. I don't know what to do. I love him so much. I don't know what to do. As if we didn't have enough problems. I don't know what to do. Oh God, why us? What have we done to deserve all of this? I don't know if I can go on. I don't know what to do.

My sister, Nawal, comes into my room. She brings me soup. I hate her cooking. It reminds me of home. She thinks I like her cooking. Every now and then she cooks instead of Maria. I am sure Maria does not like that. I don't like that.

"Marwa is coming to stay with us again tomorrow," my sister says. "She'll be staying for a couple of weeks. Do you remember Marwa?" I hear her. I understand what she says. She still thinks I have lost all my marbles. "Marwa is my friend in Washington. We have been friends since we were three. Remember Marwa Habayeb? You like her."

"Of course I remember. I have AIDS, not Alzheimer's." She looks at me disapprovingly. At twenty-five, she is looking more and more like my mother. I tell her so and she under-stands me.

"I destroyed all my paintings," I say in Arabic.
"No, you didn't."
"I did too. I thought I was the one who is blind here. Didn't you see the torn-up paintings in the studio?"
"Those weren't yours. I moved your paintings to your North Beach studio."
"Then what paintings did I destroy?"
"Some godawful paintings of naked boys. Worst paintings I ever saw. They were done by a Ben something or other."
"Oh."
"Who is he?"
"A friend. A friend of Kurt's. He's dead too. Did I destroy Kurt's paintings as well?"

"No. I liked his work. I took it over to the other studio with the good paintings."

"Oh."

———

I wish I could write better. I have never been able to write anything because I don't trust my writing.

I have had many ideas which could not translate well into painting. I wanted to write them down. I never really did. I just did not have a good command of the written word.

When I first started seeing my friends die, I wanted to write a book where all the characters died in the beginning, say in the first twenty-five pages or so. I never went beyond the incipit, which I thought was a damn good one. *Death comes in many shapes and sizes, but it always comes.* I thought it was great. I wanted to make sure death and sex were associated. Look at the words *shapes, sizes,* and *it always comes.* Sexual allusions galore.

I showed it to Scott. He said I should stick to painting. I guess he thought my incipit was insipid. He did not like the idea of my book. He said one could rarely write a book about death without being sentimental. He thought only Danielle Steel could write a book about the ravages of the AIDS epidemic and get away with it.

He did like my idea of a book about Jesus meeting Mohammad— that is, the real Mohammad, the last prophet, not me. I never wrote that either.

I miss Scott.

I sit in a house in the mountains in Lebanon. I look through the window to see the Mediterranean. I see a mist covering everything below, a sumptuous, exquisite mist. It is calm and serene. I feel so safe. I feel so secure.

I hear the sound of water. I cannot figure where it is coming from. The mist comes closer, pure white. The sound of the water is coming from the mist. I am confused. The rolling mist comes closer. I begin to see waves. The mist is water. I see patches of blue. The waves grow bigger. The sound grows louder. I wonder if the Mediterranean can reach this high. The waves get darker. A darker blue.

I worry. How could this be happening? The waves get bigger. An even darker blue. They cover the house. It is storming. Water submerges the house. It is coming in. Water, water, everywhere. Cracks in the ceiling appear and water comes in. Through the windows. Through the doors. The house shakes. The water is all enveloping. It is rough. I panic.

A process of genocide is being carried out before the eyes of the world.

Pope John Paul II told the world that in 1989, when the Syrians were shelling Christians in East Beirut. A rumor started circulating that the Pope was coming to Beirut. He wanted to suffer with the Lebanese. The amazing part of this story is everyone believed it. Christians and Muslims alike believed the Pontiff cared enough to make a statement with his physical presence. The Pole never showed up, of course. The Syrians annihilated the Christians. Lebanon became a Syrian state. The Pope did brunch with Ronnie and Nancy.

———

Much had changed in Beirut since Samir left. Much had remained the same. He returned for the first time in the early eighties. He spent most of his vacation at the Coral Beach. The Coral was one of the better beach clubs in the city.

On one occasion, he was swimming in the pool. He noted the usual lineup of sunbathers circling the pool. Very few, if any, went anywhere near the beach. Very few, if any, actually went in the pool. The club's clientele consisted mainly of women who socialize. The sunbathers were all perfectly tanned. All wore designer bathing suits, never too revealing, but always alluding to something more.

While he was swimming, the sound of a huge explosion rocked the club. Cabanas shook. Some of the empty beach chairs moved. He panicked. His first reaction was to dive underwater. He realized that was silly since whatever happened had already happened. He figured it must be one of those car bombs he kept hearing about. Nobody around him budged.

One woman finally sat up on her recliner. She lifted the designer sunglasses from her face, looked around her, and said, "That was close." She repositioned her glasses, lay back down.

———

Kurt was one of those people who believed in embracing the virus. He felt it had a positive impact on his life. "Crisis awakens," he used to say. *Crisis awakens*. He thought people walked around comatose. He said the virus woke him up. He quit his job in 1986, the day he found out he was positive. He embarked on a self-exploration program. He wanted to self-actualize, he always said. He loved attending personal growth workshops.

I found his I-love-my-virus attitude irritating as hell. Luckily, he was not the proselytizing type. Even I had to admit, whether he embraced the fucking virus or not, the transformation was incredible. When I first met him, he was a mousy troglodyte who worked as a headhunter. How the hell he kept his job was beyond me since I could not imagine him selling anything to anybody. By the time he died, he was a fairly well-respected artist in the city. His memorial filled Grace Cathedral with friends and admirers.

———

I found a sentence in an old notebook:

In the commemoration of death, I unearthed myself.

———

I hate Yoko. I do not know her. I do not even like the Beatles. I find them sappy. I was born the year they broke up, so they are not part of my history. I do not blame her for breaking them up. To tell you the truth, I think she did the world a favor if she was the cause of the dissolution.

I hate Yoko because my father's catch phrase was "Damn that Yoko." I grew up damning Yoko. Whenever he was surprised, annoyed, or angry, he would use his favorite aphorism.

I was four when my mother served stewed okra for dinner. It looked revolting. I told my mother I hated it. She insisted I eat it. It was good for me. Dad consoled me by reminding me we had rice pudding for dessert, my favorite. I stared at the slimy okra. "Couldn't we send it to the starving children in Egypt?" I asked. Dad laughed, but Mom did not. "You have to eat it," she said. "Damn that Yoko," I said. Dad almost fell off the chair laughing. My mother pretended to be upset, but I saw her smile. "Damn that Yoko." Louder, each time I repeated it. I stood up on the chair, screamed, "Damn that Yoko." Mom, openly laughing now, sat me down. "You still have to eat your dinner, champ." Dad tousled my hair. I ate the okra. It didn't taste too bad.

I was five when I first saw my mother cry. Everything was fine. We were going to visit my grandparents. I was sitting on Grandma Salwa's lap when she said, "Will you kiss Grandma Nabila for me?" I agreed. The heater wheezed. The room was large, yet warm. I thought she was cold. "Are you wearing the present I gave you last year?" she asked me. "Sure," I said. I took out the gold cross from under my sweater and showed it to her. "Can we give it to your mother to keep in a safe place?" "I won't lose it," I said. She wheezed, like the heater. "I know that, Makram. I know that. You're a big boy now. You wear this when you are proud of it. These days, it is nothing to be proud of. We have to keep it safe until you can be proud of it again." I didn't understand what she meant, but I let her remove the cross. I heard my mother gasp behind me. When I looked back, I saw her walk towards us like a queen, but she was crying. She kissed Grandma Salwa and told her she loved her. She took off her gold chain, which said Allah in Arabic, and took my cross from my grandmother. My dad gave her his cross. He carried me and said, "One day soon we can be proud of wearing them again." My mother and grandmother hugged and cried. I was very confused. "Damn that Yoko," I said. "Damn that Yoko," my father repeated, laughing.

We lived in a big house, in the town of Ba'abda. It was where the president lived. My father did not like him. From the front side of the house, I could see all of Beirut. From the back, I had an unobstructed view of the woods. It was my playpen. On a clear morning, in February of 1978, my father and I had just taken a bath together. We both dried off. The Beatles' song "Revolution" was playing on the record player. Mom was making breakfast. The music was loud. We were singing right along. I stood on a stool, but I was still much shorter than my dad. I combed my hair. He combed his blond hair back into its usual ponytail. "We all want to change the world . . ." We sang together. He lathered his face and I wanted to do the same thing. He covered my face in lather. I watched him shave. I got to "alright" in the verse, "Don't you know it's gonna be . . . alright," when the shell exploded in the woods. The house shook. The music stopped. The foam on my face was red. A piece of shrapnel had flown through the window and hit my father in the throat. Blood was everywhere. My father sat on the floor holding his throat. Mom rushed screaming into the bathroom. He couldn't breathe. I kept screaming, "Damn that Yoko," but he wouldn't laugh.

The Syrians killed my father, but I blame Yoko.

———

Even diseases have lost their prestige, there aren't so many of them left. . . . Think it over . . . no more syphilis, no more clap, no more typhoid . . . antibiotics have taken half the tragedy out of medicine.

The quote is by Louis-Ferdinand Céline, a writing doctor who died in 1961. I found it in a book of his essays edited by that fucker, Buckley, in 1989.

AP 14 Apr 96 22:02 EDT V0272

Israel Spurs Lebanon Exodus

BEIRUT, Lebanon (AP)—Israeli aircraft bombarded guerrilla strongholds in Beirut and southern Lebanon on Sunday, doubling the tide of refugees to 400,000 and provoking guerrilla vows to turn northern Israel into a "fiery hell."

Undaunted by Israel's four-day aerial barrage, Hizballah guerrillas hit northern Israel with rockets that came crashing down every 20 minutes for seven hours. One person was wounded and an empty school and other property were damaged.

Israeli jet fighters knocked out a Beirut power relay station, cutting electricity to many parts of the capital and its suburbs. It was the first deliberate attack on an economic target since Israel launched its offensive against the Iranian-backed Hizballah on Thursday.

Hizballah's Al-Manar television station showed about 50 would-be suicide bombers with explosives strapped to their chests— members of a "brigade of martyrdom-lovers" ready to avenge the Israeli attacks.

About 190,000 panicked Lebanese residents fled the southern port city of Tyre and 41 surrounding villages Sunday after Israel warned it would attack the area at sundown to drive out guerrillas.

"Whenever Israel and Hizballah are mad at each other, we pay the price," said Kassem Reda Ali, a 68-year-old farmer fleeing his home for the second time in three years.

"Why prolong our agony?" he asked. "Just throw us in the sea."

Zayneb Duhainy, a Shiite Muslim housewife, hugged her 4-year-old son and blamed the United States for not intervening to stop the Israeli offensive.

"When Kuwait was invaded, the U.S.A. rushed to its aid," she said. "Are the Kuwaitis human beings and we're animals?"

About 400,000 refugees—more than half of the population of southern Lebanon and about one-tenth of the country's people—were headed north Sunday for the relative safety of Beirut.

The mass exodus was reminiscent of the last major Israeli strike against Hizballah, a weeklong offensive in July 1993 that killed 147 Lebanese, wounded about 500, and uprooted half a million people.

With huge numbers of people on the move Sunday, Israeli aircraft struck again.

The southern market town of Nabatiyeh and southeastern villages took the brunt of the raids, which destroyed several houses belonging to Hizballah commanders.

Israeli aircraft also struck near Tyre, hitting a civil defense ambulance and injuring four paramedics. It was Israel's second helicopter raid on an ambulance in as many days. Saturday's attack killed six civilians, including three children.

The recent violence has engulfed not only the long-tense South but the capital, too, for the first time since Israel invaded Lebanon in 1982 to expel Palestinian guerrillas.

With elections just six weeks away, Prime Minister Shimon Peres of Israel has hit hard at Hizballah in an effort colored partly by a desire to prove he will not let peacemaking compromise Israel's security.

At a weekly Cabinet meeting on Sunday, Peres said Israel's military campaign was open-ended, but he added: "If the Hizballah ceases its attacks, we will cease ours."

Lebanese Prime Minister Rafik Hariri called Israel's attacks in Lebanon unjustified.

"The Lebanese people are paying the price of Peres' election and that's not right," he said in Paris, where French leaders were planning to send their foreign minister to the Middle East to try to mediate a cease-fire.

Hizballah issued a statement saying it would continue firing rockets on northern Israeli towns and vowed to turn the area "into a fiery hell."

Twenty rockets fell on more than a dozen settlements in less than seven hours, and the guerrillas said they had expanded the range of their attacks to Safed, five miles south of the border.

Most casualties from the latest round of fighting have been Lebanese civilians. Israel says guerrillas were putting civilians in harm's way by hiding among them, while Lebanon maintains Israel is deliberately targeting civilians.

———

Steve was the epitome of the angry young man. He was one of the founders of ACT UP in San Francisco. I believe it was his anger that kept him alive for so long. He always said he wanted to stay alive long enough to bite Reagan's nose off. Steve was one of the first to be diagnosed with the disease. The acronym at the time was GRID, Gay Related Immune Deficiency. He was part of the hepatitis study of the late seventies. The blood they drew from him then turned out to be positive. Yet he went on living, baffling the experts.

Kurt convinced him he should attend a workshop with Louise Hay. Kurt felt Louise would be able to help him resolve his anger issues. For two days, Kurt and Steve listened to Louise explain about creating one's own reality. Kurt kept expecting Steve to get upset during the workshop. It did not happen. Steve absorbed it all. Louise explained making things happen in your life. She always found parking spaces, she said, because she created reality. On Sunday afternoon, the last day of the workshop, Louise began talking about the possibility of dying. She said if you were not creating your own reality, and it was time for you to die, you should accept it. Do not fight it, she said.

At this point, Kurt noticed that Steve stood up. He interrupted Louise. "Excuse me," Steve said. "Let me see if I have this straight." He paused, placed one hand on his chin, with one finger pointing up in the universal I-am-pondering pose. "Basically what you are saying is, 'First you park, then you die.'"

Kurt burst out laughing. He took his friend's hand and walked out of the building.

———

Scott told the doctor he was better. Tests showed his T-cell counts were improving. He had more energy.

The doctor said he probably had AIDS dementia, which is why he imagined he was getting better.

When I found out, I stormed into the congenital idiot's office looking for trouble. I could not find the good doctor. My noisy entrance warned him. He did not return my phone calls either.

———

We all had what some would call a European complex. We wanted so hard to be European. This manifested itself in a couple of ways. There were those who mimicked everything European. They ate European, dressed European, watched European movies. It was a sign of sophistication if one intermixed difficult English words with the predominant French. Many of these Lebanese— let's call them Francophiles—had trouble speaking their native language, Arabic. They really had problems speaking to other Lebanese if those others were not like them, if they did not speak French fluently. Most Francophiles were Christians, but not exclusively. They even developed a relationship to America similar to what the Europeans have, an unhealthy fascination mixed with simultaneous disdain.

Another manifestation was the complete opposite. Many hated Europeans with a passion. Some tried to revive Arabism. Is-

lamic Fundamentalism was on the rise. They kidnapped Westerners.

One lone person blew up two hundred marines, while another
blew up only fifty-seven Frenchies.

———

I was reading a book about this man traveling in Lebanon. The
man went from one small village to the next. He described how
beautiful the villages were, how kind the people were. He came
into the mountains where I was born. I was so disappointed. He
described the village before my home village and then skipped
ahead to the next village. Tears welled up in my eyes. The teacher
asked me if I was sick. I told him the writer skipped my home.
The teacher explained that writers could not include everything
in a story. I understood that. I asked the teacher if there was a
book that had my home in it. He did not know. I asked my father
when I got home. He asked to see my book. He got really upset.
He told me the book was trash. It had nothing to do with Lebanon.
I almost started crying again. I liked the book. He said this book
was about a Christian Lebanon. Our village was not in it because
it was not Christian. All the villages in the book were Christian.
I didn't understand.

———

I just can't stand watching another TV movie about AIDS. Can't
they fucking get a gay man to write one of those, as opposed to the
constant crap we have to be subjected to? Jesus Christ. Those
writers have no idea.

I ask you. Did you see *An Early Frost*? If that doesn't get your
blood boiling, I don't know what will. In that stupid film, we see

how AIDS affects the guy's mother, father, sister, brother-in-law, and grandmother. There is no consideration given to the fact all this is happening to him, not them. Fuck.

———

Mr. Suleiman was driving the car. His wife was sitting next to him. His two sons, sixteen and fourteen, as well as his four-year-old daughter, were in the back. They were driving back home. It was seven o'clock, already dark. There was no one else on the road. The electricity was out as usual. On the road past Damour, they encountered two men in military fatigues, carrying machine guns. They directed the car to the side. A flying checkpoint. They ordered Mr. Suleiman out of his car. They could not have been older than his sons. They asked him to open the trunk. He did. The younger of the two opened fire on Mr. Suleiman. Sixteen bullets killed him. He fell into the trunk. They pushed his legs into the trunk and calmly locked it.

They walked into the night chatting boisterously. His wife wailed inside the car. His children sat in shock. Another car passed the noisy car. It was spared. The flying checkpoint was moving.

———

In one of his short stories, Coover takes the reader into an old village. Slowly, he brings the various characters into view, except they are all the same character. We see a funeral procession. The dead man in the casket looks exactly like the six pallbearers, exactly like the priest and his assistants, and exactly like the mourning women. They take the casket to the cemetery, interring it into its plot. We hear scratching and clawing. The dead man comes out of the ground. We see the people flee. The dead man runs after them. We notice him entering one of the houses in the village. He sees the dress and scarf of one the mourners. He puts it on. He becomes one of the mourners. Another man puts on the priest outfit, and others the pallbearers' outfits. We have the funeral procession starting again with a new, but the same, dead man. We see the cycle begin all over again.

I wish I could write short stories like that. I could describe the human condition so eloquently and succinctly.

———

December 18th, 1995
Dear Diary,

I called Samir today. He sounded strange so I asked him what was wrong. He tried to assure me everything was fine, but I knew. I figured out he was crying. When I asked him what made him cry, he admitted he was cleaning out his phone book. It brought tears to my eyes. What have we done to deserve all this? He said he had to erase out the names of a number of friends who have died. I cried as well. Both for him and me. I have done the same thing so many times. In the eighties, I would go through my phone book every year. So many friends died, so many simply moved away, emigrated. The war took a terrible toll.

He reminded me that I taught him to write only in pencil in the address book. I told him people move, and you have to keep erasing. They do move. He still has the same black leather address book I gave him when he left here. I bought two of them, one for him and one for me. I still carry mine. We have that in common.

———

I met Mohammad through Scott. I had seen him a couple of times before, but did not really meet him until I started dating Scott. Scott and I had been talking, typing to be exact, for a couple of months before we actually met face-to-face. We were both using a computer bulletin board, a BBS, called Queer Bee. I met many people, and made many friends, using that system. Scott's handle on the BBS was interesting. He called himself Bookworm. Nomenclature on the BBS was always interesting—one extrapolated a significant amount of information based on the choice of handle a person assumed. However, a disparaging or self-deprecating handle was rarely used. In normal situations calling oneself a bookworm may not be pejorative; however, this was a gay BBS, which the majority, if not all, of the men used to cruise for sex. In this case, it was the kiss of death.

Since I was not cruising for sex, or I should say cruising for sex was not necessarily my primary pursuit, or the foremost reason for conversing with other users, I talked to Scott at various times while on the BBS. I found out he used the handle because he owned a bookstore and it happened to be my favorite bookstore in the city. He, of course, loved books and had read all of my favorite books, but his favorite writers, I was ashamed to admit, I had never read, and some I had never even heard of. We found out we were the same age. When we got to know each other better, and being the type of open person that I am, I explained to him the problem with his handle. He was honestly surprised BBS users might find his handle deprecatory and said he would change it at some point. He never did.

We decided to meet after we found out we both adored the same film, *The Hunger*. I loved it because it perfectly described the human condition. The constant search for immortality, life's prerequisite of feeding on life, the theory of life being repeated patterns, and so on. He loved it for completely different reasons not the least of which was his adoration of Catherine Deneuve. The movie was playing at the Castro the following week, so we set a date.

That date changed my life.

The Deer Hunter started a trend in Lebanon. The militia fighters, particularly the Phalange, started playing Russian roulette.

I lost track of Georges when I left Lebanon in 1975. I kept up with news and gossip about him for a while. Apparently he had gotten to the point of being unable to see a picture of Arafat on TV without spitting on the screen. He cut himself once, requiring sixteen stitches in his arm, trying to punch the screen while watching a news clip with the PLO leader. It sounded like he had become deranged.

The boy I knew had died when the war started. Georges had become a killing machine.

The rumors were he became the Phalange's most ruthless killer. They said he took part in the Karantina massacre. That was in January, 1976, so he couldn't have been more than eighteen. It took a while to fit the image I had of Georges with what he had become. A neighborhood friend told me in 1978 that if Georges had seen me on the street, he would have shot me. No doubt about it.

They said Georges died in 1980 while playing Russian roulette. He was twenty-three. I still think it was plain suicide. From what I remember of him, he would not waste time. If he wanted to kill himself, he wouldn't play Russian roulette. He would just blow his head off. Then again, maybe the drugs he took changed him.

Ben was a slut. Ben was a delusional slut. His handle on the BBS was Cute Boy, but he was neither cute nor a boy, I assure you. He loved screwing minorities, mostly Asians. He wasn't exclusively a rice queen, but why quibble?

After his diagnosis, he had a lot of free time on his hands so he started visiting masseurs. One day, he told me there was this guy who had fallen madly in love with him. Of course, he was bragging. I knew he had an open relationship with his lover, but I gathered this was a little more serious than the casual fucks he indulged in. I asked him who the suitor was. It turned out he was an East Indian masseur. They had been having great sex regularly, and they even started working out together at the gym.

"Whoa," I say sarcastically. "Are you sure you are ready for such a commitment? Working out together is a big step."
"You don't understand, Kurt," he says. "This is real."
"What about Alan? What does he think of all of this?"
"He's okay with it. He knows I love him, but this is different. This is special."

It was so special that Ben started designing the masseur's ads (let's call him Corey, which isn't his real name, but I don't want to get in trouble for using his real name, which was probably fake anyway), which appeared in the weekly gay paper, the *Bay Area Reporter.* I started calling his attempts at designing Corey's ads his pimpish ways. He found that amusing.

Ben's workouts started getting more serious. He would stop by my house after working out, and he could barely move. His muscles ached. He was working out six days a week. They had hired a personal trainer to get them beefed up. I worried about his health, but he insisted he never felt better.

I noticed one day he started carrying a beeper. I sarcastically asked if it was part of his pimpish ways. He brushed me off. I wondered what a guy on disability would want with a beeper. I figured Ben wanted to feel important. A little while after that he got a cellular phone. That was really strange. He now had both a beeper and a cellular.

"Tell me the truth," I ask. "Are you Corey's pimp? Why the fuck are you carrying a cellular?"
"I'm not anybody's pimp."
"Then why are you carrying a beeper?" I insist.
"What if someone wanted to get ahold of me right away? I was at the Castro the other day going in to see *The Hunger* and I got beeped. This queen was at the pay phone and he wouldn't stop talking, so I couldn't use it to call whoever paged me. I decided to get a cellular."
"What's so important? Why are you being beeped?"

He sheepishly asked me if I had the current issue of the *B.A.R.* I gave it to him. He opened it to the escorts section. He showed me an ad with a guy's smooth torso. The headline said Preppy Top. I could not figure out what was going on. I looked at Ben and he was beaming—radiant was more like it, proud as a peacock.

"What the fuck?" I say.
"That's my beeper number you see," he says boastfully. He is about to burst at the seams, unable to stop smiling.
"Are you telling me you're the Preppy Top?" I ask.
"Yep!"

"People pay you for sex?"

"Yep." He beams.

"Oh, Jesus. You're a fucking whore."

"And I get paid for it too," he coos.

―――――

Viruses are any of various simple submicroscopic parasites of plants, animals, and bacteria that often cause disease and that consist essentially of a core of RNA or DNA surrounded by a protein coat. Unable to replicate without a host cell, viruses are typically not considered living organisms.

Not a living organism? Man, in his arrogance, decides this planet's most tenacious biotype is not a living organism.

Man is nothing more than giant genitalia for viruses.

―――――

Mohammad went to Dallas to attend the opening reception of his exhibit at the Fort Worth Museum of Modern Art. He was to stay there for only a couple of days. One of the trustees put him up at a luxurious apartment of another trustee who was out of town. The woman had left detailed notes of what he could and could not do in the apartment. He was reading the notes when he decided to make himself a strong drink. He opened the icebox to get some ice when he saw another note strategically placed inside. It said: *No national specialties with odors hard to get rid of.*

He took his bag and left for the airport.

―――――

An hour later. Arjuna and his charioteer, Krsna, on the battlefield. They are now joined by Eleanor Roosevelt, Krishnamurti, Julio Cortázar, and Tom Cruise, who looks a little lost.

ARJUNA: Can you give me a little hint? I am about to embark on the mother of all battles and you still run peripatetic dialectics by me. Could you just tell me what the purpose of life is all about?

KRSNA: What do you think I have been doing?

ARJUNA: Well, I don't get it.

ELEANOR: The purpose of life is to live it.

ARJUNA: Oh Eleanor, can you lower your voice an octave when you speak? It is so damn irritating.

KRSNA: High voice or not, the lesbian is right.

ARJUNA: Are you suggesting life has no purpose? No unity, nothing to pull all these illogical vignettes into a coherent collage? If that is the case, then how do biographers do what they do? If there is no unity, then how do the biographies of Ava Gardner or Eva Gabor make sense?

JULIO: But do we have to wait till someone dies before we find his life's unity, the sum of all the actions that define a life? The problem consists in grasping that unity without becoming a hero, without becoming a saint, or a criminal, or a

37

boxing champ, or a statesman, or a shepherd; to grasp unity in the midst of diversity, so that that unity might be the vortex of a whirlwind.

KRSNA: Why is it you humans constantly search for a deeper meaning?

JULIO: To sell books.

KRSNA: What if I told you that life has no unity? It is a series of nonlinear vignettes leading nowhere, a tale, told by an idiot, full of sound and fury, signifying nothing. It makes no sense, enjoy it.

KRISHNAMURTI: I had a vision once. It is the same vision you had when the mist turned into stormy waters in the hills of Lebanon. I was standing watching a mother washing her infant in the Ganges. She looked angelic as she washed her naked son. When she was done, she bit his head off.

JULIO: Ah. You are suggesting that life is the struggle between feelings and the intellect.

KRISHNAMURTI: Not at all, I am suggesting that the purpose of life is to understand it.

ARJUNA: Explain it to me then. You are closer to God. You are a guru. What is the purpose of life?

KRISHNAMURTI: I am not a guru. I am not a guru.

KRSNA: My dear fellow, you have to realize that when you abnegated your guruship, when you gave it all up, you became the greatest guru of them all.

TOM: I am not a homosexual. I am not a homosexual.

ELEANOR: Oh, shut up!

ARJUNA: I wish someone could explain the purpose of life to me.

KRSNA: There is none. Go out and kill your cousins.

ELEANOR: Live your life.

KRISHNAMURTI: And stay away from books by David Leavitt or Deepak Chopra.

JULIO: Here, here.

———

Solitude is the playfield of Satan. I was having nightmares at night and panic attacks during the day. The various news reports about the mysterious disease striking gay men were having an unsettling effect on me.

I always thought if I became a famous artist, I would be less lonely. It proved to be the complete opposite. The response to my first show at Heller was surprisingly sensational. At twenty-one, I was called the voice of a new generation. The review in the *San Francisco Chronicle* had the headline, Great Debut for Gay Artist. I could not sleep that night. I was terror-stricken. I called home, but the maid relayed a message from my father saying I was never to call back. How they had heard so quickly, I was never to find out.

I was alone. A piece of my heart was forcibly taken out. Eradicated. Expurgated. Obliterated. Emasculated.

I called Scott and asked him to move in. He packed his belongings and moved out of his apartment in less than twenty-four hours. We became even more inseparable. We became one word, Mohammad and Scott, Scott and Mohammad. One person. One life. One love.

———

In America, I fit, but I do not belong.
In Lebanon, I belong, but I do not fit.

———

It is Thanksgiving. The year is 1996. James sits alone. The first year he is completely alone. In 1982 he decided not to go back home for Thanksgiving. A group of friends formed the We Are Family group. There were seven of them that year. They came over for a Thanksgiving dinner at his house. When dinner was over, they played Sister Sledge's disco hit full blast. They played that song at every Thanksgiving since. Through the years the group got bigger with lovers joining in. Through the years the group got smaller with friends dying. This was supposed to be the fifteenth Thanksgiving. Not a single member of the group, not one person who had had Thanksgiving dinner at his house is left alive. Not a single member of the group ever reached his fortieth birthday.

James is thirty-nine. James sits alone.

Of all the nicknames I have been called, Mo is the one name I completely abhorred.

For your perusing pleasure, I submit, translated and unedited, a brief editorial from the Swiss *Tages-Anzeiger* newspaper:

QUOTE

Why Beirut and not Damascus?

Shimon Peres attacks Lebanon and bombs Beirut claiming he is aiming at Hizballah bases. He hopes, thereby, to brighten his image and strengthen his position in view of the upcoming elections. All his victims will leave cold an Assad who does not himself hesitate to sacrifice anyone to keep his power. Why didn't the Prime Minister of Israel attack Damascus or Teheran directly? Lebanon is an easy target: it cannot respond. The Nobel Peace Prize winner Peres has innocent defenseless civilians killed. He pursues a political goal by hitting people who are completely powerless in this entire affair. When Assad, when the Iranians, when the Islamic groups, when the Palestinians, act with the same methods, we call this terrorism.

UNQUOTE

Well, guess who won the election after all?

Tim wanted to drive. He had been cooped up in his studio apartment for two weeks. He picked Kurt up at his flat.

"You're looking good," Kurt said.

"Thanks. I feel better."

"So what are we going to see?" Kurt asked.

"I wanted to see *Dead Man Walking,* but I don't think I'm up for a serious movie. We're going to see *Babe.*"

"That's a good idea. I wouldn't mind seeing it again. We don't have to watch the whole thing, okay? If you get tired we can leave."

"I'll be fine."

"You look like you put on some more weight since last week."

"Three pounds. The Megace is really working. I'm eating normally again."

"That's great."

"I probably have to stop taking it soon."

"Why?"

"I don't want to gain too much weight."

"Jesus. You're not serious?"

"Look, just because you don't care about your weight, doesn't mean I don't have to."

"Reality check! Reality check! Let's see. You have no T-cells. You've lost over twenty pounds in the last three months. But now you're worried about being fat?"

"You're fucking grumpy tonight. Gee, Tim, we haven't gone out to a movie in a while. Let's do that so I can insult you tonight, Tim. What's the matter, Tim? Can't I—"

"If you stop taking Megace, I will kill you myself."

"Okay. Okay, Mr. Grumpy."

"I swear you're crazy."

"And you're fat."

My sister is massaging my feet. It feels really good. They swell quite a bit these days.

"Are you going to dry my feet with your hair?" I ask.
"Probably not, but I am sure Maria would love to," she replies.
I smile.
"He hasn't completely lost his sense of humor, I see." She smiles.

———

I am back in Beirut with my cousin. It is 1974, but we are the same age we are now. We decide to go see our families. I worry whether I will be able to see myself, meet myself when I was four-teen. The science fiction writers are wrong. It is possible to go back in time and meet yourself. Our family does not recognize us, but they do welcome us into the fold. My cousin is happy. This is where he wants to be. He no longer has any responsibilities. He can drink and be merry. He even gives his fourteen-year-old self a sip of his beer.

I meet myself. I am proud of my younger self. I am mature, stu-dious, and precocious. I realize I have a couple of options. I can stay in Beirut and teach my fourteen-year-old self everything I know. I can guide myself. On the other hand, I could go to San Francisco and try to stop the AIDS epidemic. Probably nobody will believe me, but I can try. My cousin, already tipsy and hav-ing a grand old time, asks me to stay. My parents, good people that they are, tell me I am welcome to stay in their house. I decide to go to San Francisco and take myself with me. I can teach myself to be human in San Francisco. It would be an educational expe-rience.

If we are suffering illness, poverty, or misfortune, we think we shall be satisfied on the day it ceases. But there too, we know it is false; so soon as one has got used to not suffering one wants something else.

Simone Weil told me that. Simone, darling, get yourself some Prozac. Enough is enough. That's what I said to her. Do you realize if antidepressants were available fifty years ago, the existentialists could have been happy? We would have been spared reading so many dull books.

———

March 26th, 1994
Dear Diary,

My daughter surprised me tonight. She had a costume party to go to and dressed up as a Pink Panther, a member of the militia, not the cartoon character. Some years ago, one of the myriad of militias which sprang up in Beirut decided to differentiate itself by wearing a unique uniform. I have no idea who their fashion coordinator was. The uniform was the regular camouflage pattern except the colors were of the bright pink variety, topping it off with a pink beret. It would have been hilarious if the militia was not one of the more violent ones. We started calling them the Pink Panthers even though they preferred *Die Rosenkavaliers*.

Whoever decided on those uniforms was obviously not a woman. It isn't simply the idea that pink is not a color one associates with terror. Any woman would tell you pink fades really fast when washed. I doubt the militiamen had ever heard of a warm wash, cold rinse cycle. Within a month, the uniforms looked like regular camouflage uniforms washed with a red shirt which bled, from Pepto-Bismol to mud in less than two washing cycles.

My daughter said she paid one dollar for the whole uniform, the pants, jacket, and beret, at a discount store. One dollar. That's all that is left of that militia. They came into our world suddenly, killed tons of people, and disappeared just as suddenly as they appeared. I still have no idea who they were, what party they belonged to, or what they were fighting for. It's probably better that way.

———

I wake to the most beautiful music in the world. I hear her voice softly singing in the dark. It is always dark now. The violin is playing. Is it two violins? I know this music. I know I know this music. I can't place it. I can't think straight anymore.

That voice is heavenly. I would stay alive for that voice. I would live for that lovely voice. It is divine. I know this music. I can't understand why my mind is disappearing. I love this music.

The violin repeats the melody. The second violin repeats after the first. Or is it a viola? It must be Bach. So many times He has saved me.

I remember the short film *RSVP*. A man who died of AIDS leaves a request at a classical radio station. His friends and parents listen to the song and cry. I can't remember the song. Was it Berlioz? I do remember it was Jessye Norman singing. It was a lovely song, but not divine. This is divine. It must be Bach.

It must be Bach.

"James?" I ask.

"I'm here," James replies softly. He takes my hand.

"Who is singing?"

"Kathleen Battle. It's from *The Bach Album* with Itzhak Perlman. You used to have it on all the time while painting."

"Bete Aber Auch Dabei."

"I am sorry, Mo. I didn't understand that."

"My German is awful. That was the name of the song which just finished. Please play it again."

"Sure thing."

"Do you know what she is singing?" I ask.

"It's a mass of some sort."

"It's a prayer:
'Yet pray, even while
in the midst of keeping watch!
In thy great guilt
beg the Judge for patience,
and He shall free thee from sin
and make thee cleansed.' "

The violins come back again.

I went to a couple of Catholic churches when I found out I was positive. I wanted confession. The truth was I wanted absolution. I talked to a priest and asked him what the procedure was for confessing. He asked if I was a Catholic. I told him I was a Muslim. He looked at me funny. He said I could not get absolution if I were a Muslim.

The voice comes back again. It is divine. She is talking directly to God.

"James?"

"I'm here," James replies softly. He takes my hand.

"I want to die."

"Okay."

———

Ox sat. I bet you don't know what ox sat is.

Oxygen saturation. That's what it is. There is a new language we use these days. I mean, who knew what a T cell was ten years ago? Now it's in common use. Ten years from now, when everybody is having trouble breathing from PCP or CMV in their lungs, ox sat will be in common use too.

I bet you don't know what a picc line is.

———

July 4th, 1967

Dear Diary,

This is without a doubt the worst day of my life. It looks like we have to go back to Beirut. My husband can't take it here in Washington anymore. The head of the department at Georgetown insulted him. He called him a camel jockey. I would assume an educated man would know there are no camels in Lebanon. The worst thing was our neighbor called me names today. Celebrating their independence by insulting the foreigner. They have such bad manners over here.

I guess it is a good thing we are leaving. They fight a war over there, but it brings out the bad sides of people over here. I still can't believe Walter Cronkite. Jerusalem is liberated. "Jerusalem is liberated," he kept repeating. It was as if he or his family were leading the way. Liberated from whom? Arabs have lived in Jerusalem for as long as Jerusalem existed. Liberated? They keep treating us as if we are barbarians. Jews or Christians, these Europeans come occupy our lands and then they have the gall to say they are liberating Jerusalem.

It's a good thing we are leaving. Beirut is a much better place to raise the kids.

———

Picasso used to say that at twelve years old he was able to draw like Raphael, but it took years of hard work and dedication to train himself to draw like a child. As usual, with that lovable son of a bitch, he was lying. Lies, lies, lies. He never drew like Raphael, not at twelve, sixteen, twenty-one, forty, or sixty. He was a damn good draftsman, but he was never a Raphael. I love him.

On the other hand, when I was twelve I could draw better than Picasso. I always wished I could have met him to tell him that. The day he died, I was thirteen.

Like most children I was drawing at an early age. I was definitely a prodigy. By the age of four, I was able to draw anything I saw, realistically. By the age of six, I was copying drawings of the masters.

My mother was always proud. My father considered art to be nothing more than a pleasant hobby. He kept suggesting I attempt a more masculine hobby. I was never effeminate, but I definitely was not masculine enough for my father. In his mind, any intellectual pursuit, let alone an intuitive pursuit like drawing, was effeminate. It is no wonder none of my four older brothers went beyond a few years of college.

I was seven when my father decided to do his fatherly thing. He asked me to show him my drawings. I was nervous as I showed him my work. He looked at my copies of the masters and said, "This is good, but how come you always draw the men? I think you should draw some of the women as well. Come back and show me when you have drawn some women."

I ran into my room knowing exactly what to draw. I had seen a copy of Goya's *Nude Maja.* I drew a damn good copy of the woman lying down on the sofa. I was not able to get a good face since the reproduction was so small. I decided to improvise. I did a very good drawing of my mother's face into Goya's *Nude Maja.* I ran out of the room and showed it to my father.

I never saw his hand coming. He had turned beating his children into an art form. He slapped my face only once. That was probably because I ended up on the other side of the room by force of the blow. My mother came running into the room, and he threw the drawing in her face. He left the room saying, "Your son is a pervert."

It is true. I am a pervert. A pervert who sold a 60 by 80 called *My Mother as the Nude Maja* for $300,000 in the mid-eighties at Franklin Gallery on Fifty-seventh Street. Where was that son of a bitch then?

I was seven then. I didn't know any better. I never showed my drawings again for a very long time.

———

My mother and I are in the back seat of a huge black limousine. The driver is a bald, husky man. It is nighttime. I start kissing my mother. I begin to make love to her. I lift her evening dress and penetrate her. The driver is watching the sex through his rearview mirror. "Don't I get any?" he asks. I realize he turns me on. I leave my mother and get into the front seat while the limousine is still moving. I unbutton his fly and start sucking him. He is gratified while my mother sits in the back of the limousine, unsatisfied.

———

I woke up to the sound of my sister. She was on the phone. She was crying. I gathered she was talking to my mother. My father must have been out of the house.

The feeling of guilt is overpowering at times. I have caused such pain.

She still refused to talk to me. He still ran her life.

Well, fuck her.

———

I remember his eyes the most. There was nothing like them. Nothing. I am not sure what it was. I kept thinking maybe God was trying to punish me. His eyes were unforgettable. I was thirteen when I first met him, 1973. It seemed everything which had happened to me before then had been in preparation for that meeting. His eyes were the first thing I noticed about him.

I had wanted to meet him for about a year before it actually happened. After all, he was a legend at my school. The only boy who was ever expelled from our school for nonacademic reasons. I guess if he was better academically, they would have found a way not to expel him. Then again, maybe not. Although he was three years older than I, he was only one class ahead. His exploits were celebrated. It is said he once hung Mr. Murphy, the English teacher from New Zealand, on a coat rack. Luckily, I never had to take Murphy, who had a reputation of being a complete creep, but had Johnson, an American from Iowa.

I met him on a small street, two blocks north of Hamra Street. I was with my friend, Jamal, and he was with his friend, Shaddy, who happened to be Jamal's cousin. They were sitting outside Shaddy's building, with a cassette player blaring. He was accompanying the music, or I should say he was playing lead guitar on his acoustic guitar, which may have had something to do with what the cassette player was playing.

The music playing was Chicago's third album. It was a cassette, but I was surprised to hear it. I had all their albums, but I had to get them from the States. No CBS or RCA records were allowed legally in Beirut. It was not such a big deal since few artists I liked were on those labels. The biggest star on CBS was Bob Dylan, but his nasal voice was a big turnoff in Lebanon. Still, I heard one could get those records from some stores for only a little extra. Since my uncle still lived in the States, I usually got whatever I wanted.

We were introduced. I have to say I fell head over heels in love. He was gorgeous. His eyes were blue. That is not altogether rare in Lebanon, but I had never seen anybody that handsome with eyes that color before. I got so nervous, I did not know what to say. He ignored Jamal and me, and asked Shaddy if he liked the music. Shaddy said it was okay, but not great. I don't know what came over me. If I didn't say anything, I would regret it for the rest of my life.

"It is great music. Not as great as their live album, or some of the later ones, but it is a great album."

"You've heard the live album?" he asked me.

Ecstasy. Exhilaration. Euphoria. I said exactly the right thing. I was practically panting, but had to sound nonchalant.

"Live at Carnegie Hall? Sure. I have that album. I have all of Chicago's albums."

"Wow. That's great. Can I borrow them?"

It was just him and me. He was talking only to me.

"I guess so. I don't usually lend my albums out, but if you promise to take care of them, I can let you have them for a while."

"Great. When can I come over to get them?"

Come over. He was going to come over.

"I should be home by six."

"Where do you live?"

"Ras Beirut. I live in the building next to Marroush. Fourth floor."

"Okay. I'll be there at around seven. I can have a look at what albums you have."

My head was spinning.

"It's been great talking to you, Karim," I said. "I have heard so much about you."

"I'll see you later this evening, Samir." He beamed.

That is how it all started.

Death comes in many shapes and sizes, but it always comes. No one escapes the little tag on the big toe.

The four horsemen approach.

The rider on the red horse says, "This good and faithful servant is ready. He knoweth war."

The rider on the black horse says, "This good and faithful servant is ready. He knoweth plague."

The rider on the pale horse says, "This good and faithful servant is ready. He knoweth death."

The rider on the white horse says, "This good and faithful servant killed his best friend. Let him suffer."

The testy rider on the white horse leads the other three lemmings away.

My eyes hurt. They hurt from the inside. A constant throbbing.

———

March 17th, 1987
Dear Diary,

Americans make fun of us. They mock us. My son told me they even had a comedy skit about us on *Saturday Night Live*. I am not sure what that is. I think it is a program on television which mocks things. They make fun of us all the time, it seems. They think we are all crazy, maybe even degenerate. The only way they make our suffering palatable is by envisioning us as less than human. We are human. What happened to us could happen to anyone. They refuse to see it. They think all of us just go around killing each other. My son said they had a film showing all the bullets flying over at night and the announcer says in a serious voice, "Come visit us in Beirut, where it is Fourth of July every night." I don't think that's funny.

———

The woman comes up to me. I notice the museum director stiffen. I guess she must be a trustee.

"Mr. Momad, I wonder if you can answer a question for me." Her voice is nasal, irritating. "It's Mohammad, Mrs. Winters," the director says. "It's his first name."

I look at her. I see no need to reply. The director is nervous, but is unsure what his role is in such situations. She keeps going.

"You are a gay artist, aren't you?" Pause. Wait for a response. None coming. She continues, "I was wondering what you think of Keith Haring's work."
"He's dead," I say.

The director chuckles and tries to say something, but she keeps going.
"Yes, I know that. I would like to know what you think of his work."
"It's okay," I say.

The director is trying to figure where this conversation is going. He fidgets.

"That's what I think too," she adds. "I don't know what the big deal about his work is. It's not bad, but really, what is the big deal? How come he became such a big name all of a sudden? Unlike your paintings, which are truly magnificent, by the way, I find his work to be more decorative, more illustrative. Don't you agree? What was the seminal work that catapulted him? Where is his tour de force? Which painting is his chef d'oeuvre? Now tell me, what do you think is his one work which you can honestly say made him into a superstar artist?"
"The AIDS diagnosis?"

The director drops his champagne glass.

The museum goes silent.

———

Once upon a time there was an island visited by ruin and inhabited by strange peccant creatures.

"It's a sad place," I say, "and too much like my own life."
He nods. "You mean, the losing struggle against inscrutable blind forces, young dreams brought to ruin."

"Yes," I tell Coover, "my young dreams are gone. I lost the struggle a long, long time ago."

———

During the war, rumors were rampant suggesting downtown Beirut was not being rebuilt because they found archeological treasures when the buildings were razed, a romantic notion and much more pleasant than the truth. Like most rumors, it was based partially on truth. They did find archeological treasures, from Phoenician urns and pottery to remnants of the Roman law school, the pride of Roman Berytus, from Macedonian spears to Islamic tiles. They found the remains of five thousand years of successive civilizations. According to *The New York Times*, the finds confirmed the fact that Beirut was founded as early as 3000 B.C., before Jerusalem, Athens, Damascus, or any other current capital. Only Jbeil, once known as Byblos, another Lebanese city north of Beirut, is older. The latter is the oldest city in the world, continuously inhabited for seven thousand years.

The archeologists had little time to dig through what was found. When the war stopped, the government, run by some of the richest men in the world, which included the militia leaders, wanted to make their money developing downtown Beirut. They had no time for old crap.

A girl led one of the expeditions. She looked to be no more than fourteen or fifteen, but she was actually nearing thirty, not typical for a Lebanese. Whatever her age, she was an experienced archeologist, a Harvard Ph.D., and a veteran of many archeological digs. She realized her government did not care. She attempted to involve the press, but that proved futile. After the war, the press was the government. She attempted to involve her peers at Harvard. They became interested at first. They reneged as it became obvious which American corporations were involved in rebuilding downtown Beirut and where the money was coming from.

She would try to salvage whatever she could before they brought in the bulldozers. She was working in a belowground site when she uncovered a death mask. She showed it to the rest of her team. At the moment she held it up, a government employee screamed they had ten seconds to get out. A sewer was opened intentionally to drive them out. They smelled the water before it hit them. The force of the shitty water pulled the death mask away. Within a minute, the team was floating among excrement. They could not save anything. The bulldozers had come.

———

"Habibi?"

"I'm here, dear." It was frightening. His face was hideous. The most beautiful boy in the world was gone, the swan into the ugly duckling. The KS was feeding on Scott's face. Omophagia.

He looked at his face in the mirror. Purple splotches everywhere.

"How are you feeling?"

"Fine," he said. "I always wondered what it felt like to be a blueberry muffin."

———

FROM: BOURMA@ESTE.ON.NET
DATE: FRI, 22 MAR 1996 00:50:47 GMT
SUBJECT: TO MY FELLOW CHRISTIANS

There have been many things said about who are the true Lebanese on this service. Most of you have an opinion as to what makes a Lebanese and whether we are Arabs. I want to clear up some misconceptions. I am writing this letter to all our Maronite friends in hopes of ending the confusion about our history. Hopefully after reading this, we will be able to stand up for who we are. I will show you why we are the true Lebanese.

We are the true Lebanese because we are the only descendants of the Phoenicians, the only indigenous people of Lebanon. Everybody else came after that. We were in Lebanon for as long as anybody can remember, at least seven thousand years because that is when the Phoenicians established the city of Byblos. We established all the cities in Lebanon—Beirut, Sidon, Tyre, and Tripoli. We gave the world the alphabet. We gave the world the color purple. The Phoenicians were the most well respected people in their time.

Lebanon was conquered by most of the great empires of antiquity. We were under the Persian empire in the sixth century B.C., and the Hellenistic Seleucid kingdom (which Alexander the Great conquered) in the fourth century B.C. That was followed by the Roman empire. We were baptized as Christians in the second century when we fell under the Byzantine empire. Then we were under Islam in the seventh century, but try as they might, the Muslims were never able to conquer the mountains because of the rough terrain and because the Christians fought valiantly. Most of the Muslims settled in the coastal cities and the Beka'a valley. In the eleventh century, the Druze came to Lebanon, and the Christians allowed them to settle in some villages in the mountains.

Since 623, Lebanon has been an unwilling part of various Islamic empires up until 1918, when we were liberated by the French. The exception was during the Crusades between 1098 and 1291, when we were under Frankish rule. As you all know, we gained full independence in 1943.

We are called Maronites because in the fifth century we had our own saint, a monk called Marun. He led his followers against various groups that tried to persecute them. The Phoenicians were Semitic and they spoke a Semitic language. With all the conquests, the Phoenicians, now Maronites, began to speak Syriac. All our church rites and liturgy were in Syriac.

In summation, Maronites are NOT Arabs, never were, never will be. We are Syrio-Aramaic. We are Phoenicians. We need to be proud of our heritage and revive it. We need to throw away the Arab shackles that everybody tries to bind us with. We are not Arabs. We are Lebanese. Lebanon is the homeland of Christians. We shall refuse to live under occupation. We will always be Christian, always Lebanese.

Just like our Lord Jesus Christ, we will rise again. We shall overcome this tragedy and conquer. We will rise again, purer and stronger, to throw out the current aggressors from OUR land. We refuse to wear the labels they give us. We will revive the Syriac language. No Christian should speak the language of our oppressors. I have not spoken Arabic since 1978. We are not Arabs. We are the true people of Lebanon.

With the true love of our Lord Jesus Christ, I bless you all.

Roger Dabbas

Rewriting history is a passion for most Lebanese. Lebanon is a mixture of races from all over Europe and the Middle East, yet everyone tries to lay claim to being the true descendants of the Phoenicians. In reality, any Palestinian, Syrian, and Jordanian may be a descendant as well. Most of the indigenous people of

Lebanon actually changed religions and alliances under each occupier. The reason is simple. It saved on taxes. The empires of the area always taxed religious minorities at a higher rate.

The name of their monk should be written as Maroun, not Marun. The stress is on the second syllable. But obviously the writer is demented. I sent him a note saying my spell checker could not recognize the word *Marun*. It came up with *manure* as an alternative, which I felt was appropriate. I received death threats. If you need further proof the writer is demented, look at when he introduces Christianity into the Roman empire. Heck, any idiot knows that Hadrian and Marcus Aurelius were still killing Christians and Jews in the second century. Those were the days.

———

Scott was handsome. Surprisingly, since he was relatively shy on the BBS. We enjoyed ourselves. We laughed during the movie when Scott pretended to faint as Deneuve made her first appearance. We went for beers and talked. We had a good time on our first date. We had a better time on our second date and ended up in my bed. He only mentioned Mo on our third date.

I have to admit I am easily impressed by celebrity. It is a weakness. I don't go crazy, I never ask for autographs, or anything silly like that. I am just impressed. I think that's human. Our culture is a celebrity-driven culture, and I am never that bad. Deep down, I'm still the boy from Bethlehem, PA, easily impressed.

The idea that Scott was Mo's best friend, but never mentioned it till that moment, was bewildering. If he were my best friend, I would surely mention it often—discreetly, I would hope, but you get the idea. I guess that's why Mo was Scott's friend and not mine.

Mo was the enfant terrible of the art world, but his reputation went beyond the art world. He was in every sense of the word a celebrity. I had met him at a couple of occasions, but never really made any contact with him. I did not understand art all that well, but I knew what I liked. I liked his realistic paintings, but never his abstract ones. I heard if an exhibit of his abstract paintings does really well, his next one is sure to be very realistic. I wanted to meet him. I pretended it was not important. I tried to find out what their relationship was. Scott assured me they were best friends. They had been living together for a while.

I finally met him. It was uneventful. He was polite. I should say he was not rude. *Polite* would be stretching it. He practically ignored me most of the time. Every time I went into his studio to talk to Scott, he would stop painting. He would not start again until I left. After a while, the novelty wore off. I stopped caring whether I saw Scott at my place or his.

I realized I loved Scott. We also realized we were not in love. About two months into our relationship we mutually decided that we liked each other too much to have sex. We became what in the "business" is called sisters.

He was coming up the stairs to my flat when he got his first attack. He had been looking haggard the past week, but nothing was seriously wrong. I can't recall exactly what happened. He was coming up the stairs. He had to stop midway because he ran out of breath. I was at the top of the stairs waiting for him to come up. I asked if he was okay. He assured me he was fine, but needed to catch his breath. He then fainted and fell down the steps.

I don't know what came over me. Instead of calling 911, I picked him up and carried him the two blocks to Davies Medical.

I had to call Mo, but I did not have his number. I could call Scott's number, but I doubted he would pick up. I could not try information since I never knew what his last name was. I don't know if anybody did. He never divulged it, to my knowledge. It finally occurred to me to call Heller, where I knew he showed his work. I left a message with them for him to call me at the pay phone.

"Kurt?" he screams into the phone.
"Hi, Mo," I say soothingly. "Calm down. He's going to be all right. He fainted coming up the steps. They're checking him now."
"I'll be right over," he says.

———

August 5th, 1996
Dear Diary,

My grandson was circumcised today. I was surprised how easily my son-in-law accepted his son's circumcision. He is Christian, Greek Orthodox. I think it is a good thing it happened. During the war, they were exchanging corpses of dead fighters on both sides. The Christians found out they had eighteen unidentified corpses. They weren't sure whether to send them to West Beirut or keep them. Bashir Gemayel told them to undress the corpses. If they were circumcised, send them to West Beirut. If they happened to be circumcised Christians, they deserved to be buried with Muslims.

———

The current definition is that of a 1981 United States presidential commission which recommended that death be defined as "irreversible cessation of all functions of the entire brain, including the brain stem," the brain stem being that part of the brain that controls breathing and other basic body functions.

We have presidential commissions to tell us what death is. God, I *love* this country.

———

Behold, I have two daughters who have not known man.

This line always fascinated me for some reason. It isn't simply because we have a father pimping his two virgin daughters. There is something poetic about it.

Behold, I have two daughters who have not known man.

It has a ring to it. I like this translation better than "Look, I have two daughters who have never slept with a man," or "Lo, I pray you, I have two daughters, who have not known anyone." Translation is so important. The new American translations of the Bible sound like a Judith Krantz novel. I would never believe the men of Sodom called to Lot, "Where are the men who came to you tonight? Bring them out to us so that we can have sex with them." But the Bible readers today prefer simple fare.

Behold, I have two daughters who have not known man.

The story of Sodom and Gomorrah is a simple story. Two angels come to visit Sodom and are invited by Lot, our hero, to stay at his house. All the men of Sodom, young and old, come to Lot's door wanting to get better acquainted with the angels. Those were the days, huh? So Lot, chivalrous host that he is, says, "I beg you, my brothers, do not act so wickedly. Behold, I have two daughters who have not known man; let me bring them out to you, and do to them as you please; only do nothing to these men, for they have come under the shelter of my roof." Isn't that precious? Let's get this straight, and I do mean straight. God tells us men fucking men is a terrible thing, but a father offering his two daughters, vestal virgins no less, to a horde of horny buggers is heroic. Now that's straight.

It gets better. God tells Lot, the pimp, to get away from Sodom, with his wife and vestal virgins, for He is to unleash His wrath. Don't look back, the angels tell them. Well, his wife does, failing to follow simple instructions, and is turned into a pillar of salt. The pimp is spared, but the wife who does not follow orders is not. Lot and his daughters end up in a cave. One day the older daughter says to the younger, "Our father is old, and there is no man around here to lie with us, as is the custom all over the earth. Let's get our father to drink wine and then lie with him and preserve our family line through our father." So the pimp gets drunk, his daughter fucks him, and he doesn't remember anything the next day. This is a common pattern among straight men. They always forget what happened the night before while they were drunk. The next night, the pimp gets drunk again and his younger daughter fucks him. All in the family and so on. Vice is nice, but incest is best.

So here we have the story of Sodom and Gomorrah. God destroys the faggots with fire and brimstone. He turns a disobedient wife into salt. But he asks us to idolize drunks who sleep with their daughters or offer them to a horny, unruly mob. This is the lesson of Sodom and Gomorrah: Homosexuals are bad.

———

"Habibi?"
"I'm here, dear."

64

"The catheter hurts."

"Do you want me to increase your dosage?"

"No, no. It's okay."

"Would you like anything?"

"Yes. A naked Julio Cortázar on a platter."

"Shit. I'm still working on Naipaul. Are you sure you wouldn't settle for Tom Cruise?"

"Ugh. I'd even take Gore Vidal first. I still have some taste."

Luckily, those were not Scott's last words, but it was a close call.

———

I idolized Karim. We moved in different circles most of the time, but we did spend time together. He played guitar in a rock band. I attended all their concerts, as well as many of their practices. The band was atrocious, but he played well. I think he enjoyed the fact the band was awful, since everybody noticed how well he played. He enjoyed having me around, being that I worshiped him.

I still consider the skiing trip we spent together as the best time of my life. His family had a chalet in The Cedars. I don't care what other people say, The Cedars was the best skiing in Lebanon. Even though Faraya and Fakra were more modern resorts, The Cedars was better, less pretentious, less nouveau riche. The Cedars itself, the village, was one of the oldest villages in Lebanon, so it had a natural charm. The resort was old money, class all the way. Anyway, what man in his right mind, if given an opportunity to ski among ten-thousand-year-old trees, would give that up to ski somewhere else just because they had better ski lifts? The Cedars was the best skiing in the world.

I had gone up as a guest of Jamal, whose family also had a chalet up there. It was Easter vacation, 1974, a few months before everything changed. We were only staying for a couple of days; both Jamal's father and Karim's had business to attend to. Those couple of days were uneventful. When the time came for us to get back to Beirut, Karim decided he wanted to stay. He actually asked me if I wanted to stay with him for another week. For whatever reason, he assumed I was hesitating. He explained to me all the fun we could have just the two of us, the parties we could attend, the extra skiing we could do, the alcohol we could drink, wink, wink. I did not need any convincing. I would have stayed with him no matter what we did.

That week was great. I discovered so much. I learned how to drink vodka. I learned how to smoke hash, how to tell the difference between the various blends. I met all these different people. We had a party every night. We also started a ritual which Karim and I would repeat practically every time we met. We would both get high out of our minds before we got to bed. We would both be in our underwear. He would play guitar just for me. I was in heaven.

I learned much that week. I figured out I was homosexual. There were times early on when I knew I liked boys, but I always thought I would outgrow the predilection. That week I figured I would never outgrow it. I also figured out I really didn't want to. At the time, I could not care less if I had sex with Karim. I loved him and that's all that mattered. He obviously liked me too. What else could a boy want? I was very happy that week.

I also learned much about other boys. Quite a few of the other boys who came to our parties were very different than I was. They were modern. They handled their drugs much easier, also their Scotch. They were more sophisticated. They spoke of Nietzsche as if he were one of their best friends. They were all teenagers like I was, but many of them seemed like a different breed. They all talked about politics like adults. They could all put together a machine gun, and then dismantle it, blindfolded.

I thought that was cool.

The war started not long after.

———

The invalid is a parasite on society. In a certain state it is indecent to go on living. To vegetate on in cowardly dependence on physicians and medicaments after the meaning of life, the right to life, has been lost ought to entail the profound contempt of society.

"Hey, Nietzsche boy," I told Friedrich. "Look who's talking about parasites on society. How many people supported your every whim and desire? You should be ashamed of yourself."

He never liked me anyway.

———

They kept Tim alive for five months more than they should have. He was a vegetable. His parents, born-again Christians, refused to have the doctors pull the plug. The machines kept forcing themselves on him. It was rape. Five months later his lungs actually exploded.

———

December 24th, 1987
Dear Diary,

What a day. We had to drive all the way to Ba'albak to buy our car back. It was our second trip. The first time, they told us our car had not arrived yet. They did have it, they assured us. It just hadn't arrived at their depot yet. Apparently it takes about five days for a stolen car to get up there. They had the gall to tell us they are trying to get more efficient. Soon it would take only three days for them to steal the car, drive it up to Ba'albak, for it to be ready to be sold back to its owners. What is this world coming to?

———

I am in a mausoleum. I climb, reaching one of the higher vaults, and enter. I have to break through an intricate spider's web. At the end of the tunnel is a bright room. I reach it to find the devil, sitting on his throne, lifelike, yet larger than life. I can feel his power. I am pulled in. He is seductive. At the end of his tail is a large penis. I am entranced.

"You can't keep your eyes off it, can you?" His voice resonates through my entire being.

A dwarf comes in. He is deaf and mute. He gestures for me to follow. I follow him out of the room. He wants to lead me through a journey of self-discovery. He directs me to a room. In the room I find my father, sitting on his throne, lifelike, yet larger than life.

———

It was a gray morning. I went into the kitchen to get my coffee. Scott had left some Danish pastries out for me. On the table, he had the paper with a headline circled in red. I sat down with my cup of coffee, and picked it up. Next to a small story on the Lebanese war, the headline read:

Reagan Wins on Budget, but More Lies Ahead.

———

(Excerpted from a letter by Mr. Kasem sent on the Internet.)

There is a historical parallel to Lebanon which, hopefully, can establish a precedent and move all Lebanese past this point of national identity as Arabs, Phoenicians, Aramaic, or whatever.

It is a well-established fact, if one looks objectively, that the very nature of Lebanon and its uniqueness lies in pluralism. Lebanon's history is that of a place of refuge, a sanctuary, for oppressed people throughout the region. It is by no means an accident one of the largest communities of Druze in the region calls Lebanon home, since the Druze sought refuge in the Lebanese mountains from persecution in Egypt. It is no accident either that the largest community of Shiite Muslims outside of Iran calls Lebanon home. Shiites, as the minority Muslim sect, were historically dominated by the majority Sunnis. It is also for this reason the largest Christian community in the region finds its home in Lebanon as well. The Maronites sought refuge in the mountains over one thousand years ago. Since then, Armenian and other Christian sects have sought refuge. Lebanon is multicultured because it is a place of refuge. It is a place where the people revel in the fact they are different from the monolithic uniformity that laps at their borders.

Because each community of Lebanon has known oppression in its history, none should oppress the other.

In recent history, there is another country which was founded as a refuge for the people of the world who were different and therefore not tolerated in their place of origin. These people flocked to this country seeking freedom of religion and expression, and they found it. However, they, too, had the same problem as the Lebanese. Since they arrived from many different places, being of many different ethnic backgrounds and religions, they, too, did not identify with their host country. Rather, they identified with their clans, with their states, or with their regions. I guess by now you have figured the historical precedent for Lebanon I am describing is the United States of America. And it is true, during the first sixty years of the country's existence no one called themselves "Americans." It was not used. The people referred to themselves as "Georgians" or "New Yorkers" or "Alabamans" or "Virginians." They never referred to themselves as Americans.

We had our civil war, as Lebanon had hers, in which one group tried to overcome the other, Northerners (Anglo-Saxons) against Southerners (Scot-Irish). Our war was more violent, and much bloodier than the Lebanese war. We, too, had the dominant international power of the day intervene on behalf of one side (the British intervened on behalf of the South in an attempt to break up the United States). The result of the civil war was the South and the British lost, and the concept of union won. It was really from that point forward that the citizens in America began to identify with the country first and referred to themselves as Americans, rather than members of one clan (read *state*) or the other. We adopted the national slogan, *E Pluribus Unum*, "From the Many There Is One." It is appropriate that Lebanon should assume this national motto. The Lebanese should not feel delegitimized because they experienced civil war. Rather, the war was a legitimizing event. It was the crucible in which the nation of Lebanon was born, in much the same way as the American

Civil War was the crucible in which the nation of America was born.

I am an American. I am also a Southerner. The South is the only region of America to have ever experienced "foreign" occupation as we were occupied by Federal troops from 1866–1872. We, in the South, did not assume the identity of our conquerors by becoming Yankees. We stayed Southerners, and to this day are proud of our unique heritage. However, we became even better Americans. To this day most of the American military is made up of Southerners. We make the finest officers and foot soldiers.

No person who engaged in, or lived through, the Lebanese Civil War—which ended, by the way, in 1976; the rest of the fighting was a proxy war of aggression executed against Lebanon by her neighbors—should feel compelled or threatened into surrendering their cultural identity as a result of the Lebanon war. Rather, a national identity should emerge, in conjunction with a cultural one. Everyone from Lebanon is a Lebanese first. Everyone passed through the war, suffered from the war, and now faces occupation because of the war and its outcome. There is a common history which weaves each community, ethnic, regional, and religious, together to form one national identity. It was the common thread of the American Civil War that did the same for America.

To be from Lebanon means you are from a place of refuge and tolerance. You share a country with people of many different backgrounds, cultural identities, and faiths. To make Lebanon like its Arabic neighbors is to deny her identity.

I agree with many of the writers that Lebanese are free to be Arabs if this is their cultural identity, and they are free to be Western if that is their cultural identity, or even Aramaic. This is the point. In Lebanon, one should be free to be different. This is the essence of being Lebanese and the essence of being American.

Wayne Kasem

———

"Can't we all just get along?" asked the modern-day philosopher with puffed lips.

———

I sent a note to Mr. Kasem asking, if the South was a hotbed of refuge and tolerance, how come they have the highest rates of gay-bashing in the world. He was not very amused. I received death threats.

———

My mother was baptized when she married my father. She had no choice. Either one of my parents had to take on the other's religion to get married. We have no civil marriage in Lebanon, only religious. Neither of them was very religious, nor were their families. I have two aunts and one uncle who had interfaith marriages. Even after my father died, and the city was divided, my mother adamantly refused to move to West Beirut, which was probably safer for her. We would have to cross to visit her parents twice a week. Grandma Salwa crossed with us on a number of occasions. For her, it was a pilgrimage, a rebellion against a state of affairs she had little control over.

My card says I am a Christian, a Maronite, to be exact. When I was ten, I asked Grandma Nabila what it meant to be Christian because I figured out she wasn't. She looked at me and said, "Well, Makram, it means you can become president of this great country of ours."

———

I never knew what attracted me to the piece. I was not into elephants. I found out from the saleslady the meditating elephant was the god of devotion. Well, devotion was not my cup of tea either. I ended up paying sixty dollars for that thing, which could not have been bigger than an inch.

I never knew why I carried that thing with me at all times. I am not much of an object person. I own nothing of value. I carried it on me at all times. I became devoted to it.

When I first found out about the virus, I was crestfallen. I never thought I would survive. I ran back to Arizona, my haven. I said, "Father, can you help me?"

Father asked me if I was sure I wanted help. I tried to convince him. Father suggested I consider a ritual, as in the old days, an offering to the gods.

I wondered what I could offer the gods. I was never very religious. I never believed in superstitious silliness.

I built a small altar in the middle of the desert. I placed my elephant on top. I prayed. I left.

The next day it stormed. I wanted my elephant back. Father said I made an offering, but if it was still there, I could take it back.

I found it. Miraculously, it was still there. Miracle of miracles.

I left Arizona for British Columbia. I stayed in a hotel room. I hid my elephant in a sock. It would have been too embarrassing to leave it in a safe deposit box. I lost it.

My health improved.

———

Addressing a virus, a war, or oneself:

"Why, with your infernal enchantments, have you torn from me the tranquillity of my early life. . . . The sun and the moon shone from me without artifice; I awoke with gentle thoughts, and at dawn I folded my leaves to say my prayers. I saw nothing evil, for I had no eyes; I heard nothing evil, for I had no ears; but I shall have my vengeance!"

From "Discourse of the Mandrake," in *Elizabeth of Egypt* by Achim von Arnim. Since a plant can't really talk, I decided to appropriate it. Sorry, Achim.

———

Christians fought among themselves again in 1989. Like their Muslim counterparts, they were more vicious eradicating their own.

General Aoun, after naming himself prime minister, wrestled control of East Beirut from the Lebanese Forces. Bodies were everywhere.

The assassin of the Lebanese Forces, Nick Akra, was found naked, in bed with his paramour, Samia Marchi, legs entwined, lips still joined. Fifty-two bullets riddled their corpses. Coitus interruptus.

———

I am at the post office, opening my mailbox. An old man is next to me getting his mail. He makes a pass at me. I am appalled. I do not like older men who seduce boys.

He puts his hand inside my pants, and touches my anus. My mind gets all fogged up.

The man leaves the post office. I follow him in a daze. I want him. He looks back to make sure I follow. I am walking about ten steps behind him. A group of teenage girls, in school uniforms, start walking in between us. They are boisterous and walking slowly. I am afraid I will lose the man. I try to go through them, but they cut me off. I try to ask them to let me by, but they are not listening to me. They talk loudly to each other, completely oblivious of me. I am getting annoyed.

I try to push my way through. One girl turns around and punches me straight in my left eye. I am no longer drugged. The fog has lifted. I am clearheaded.

I am back in Beirut. In a stable, hiding. My father walks in. He asks me what I am doing. I tell him I killed him. He is lying on the ground, dead. We both look at his body.

———

September 13th, 1993
Dear Diary,

While reading the paper today, I noticed the published names of thieves who were arrested. Before the war, the names were always Ahmad, Omar, and Ali. Now it's Pierre, Georges, and Joseph. Crime is an equal opportunity employer these days.

———

In the beginning was the Word, and the Word was with God, and the Word was Mohammad, peace be upon Him. For God so loved the world that He gave His one and only Son, that whoever believes in Him shall not perish, but have eternal life. For God did not send His Son into the world to condemn the world, but to save the world through Him. Whoever believes in Him is not condemned, but whoever does not believe stands condemned already because he has not believed in the name of God's one and only Son. For Mohammad, peace be upon Him, said God was neither a son nor a father. O People of the Book! Commit no excesses in your religion: Nor say of Allah aught but the truth. Christ Jesus the son of Mary was (no more than) an apostle of Allah, and His Word, which He bestowed on Mary, and a spirit proceeding from Him: so believe in Allah and His apostles. Say not "Trinity": desist: it will be better for you: for Allah is one Allah. Glory be to Him: (far exalted is He) above having a son. To Him belong all things in the heavens and on earth. And enough is Allah as a Disposer of affairs. One will find in the Bhagavad Gita all that is contained in other scriptures, but the reader will also find things which are not to be found elsewhere. That is the specific standard of the Gita. It is the perfect theistic science because it is directly spoken by the Supreme Personality of Godhead, Lord Sri Krsna.

Dhrtarastra said: O Sanjaya, after my sons and the sons of Pandu assembled in the place of pilgrimage at Kuruksetra, desiring to fight, what did they do?

To this I replied: A man can receive only what is given him from heaven. You yourselves can testify that I said, "I am not the Christ but am sent ahead of him."

To this the sons of Pandu replied: We do not believe you. You have AIDS dementia.

To this I replied: Those who reject Faith and keep off (men) from the way of Allah, have verily strayed far, far away from the Path.

Live with this, suckers, for I am the Word.

———

They were my girls, Marwa and Nawal. I called them the MN girls. I took care of them. They took care of me. I left them everything.

They were my girls. Like a doting parent, I took pride in every one of their accomplishments. They cowrote a number of published essays. I do not think either one of them ever wrote anything on her own. They collaborated on life.

They studied my paintings extensively. They would discuss them endlessly. They asked questions I could not answer. They wrote about my work. They became my historians, my chroniclers. They wrote essays for the catalogues of exhibits I had, including the retrospective.

They were my girls, staunch defenders against a country which wanted to obliterate me from its collective conscious. They arranged my first exhibit in Beirut, in 1995. I never thought I would see the day. The exhibit consisted solely of paintings from Lebanese collections, in Lebanon, France, and Canada. That fact alone left me dumbfounded.

They both talk about husbands. At twenty-five, they are bordering on spinsterhood by Lebanese standards. It is going to be difficult for either of them to get married, unless it is to a foreigner. In Lebanon, marriage is what I would call quasi-arranged. A boy decides he wants to get married. He tells his parents, who put the word out to the entire family. A search for the appropriate girl begins. The right family, the right background, the right culture are considered. When an appropriate girl is found, the boy and his family pay the girl and her family a visit. If the boy and girl like each other, they start dating for a couple of months, no sex, of course, only dinner and maybe a movie. They get married only if both approve of each other.

NAWb 1 ⇒ MO'S SISHr

The girls have had a number of suitors. They have not had a single date with any of them, though. My sister's trick is to simply disappear when suitors arrive. If she has not managed to leave the house before they arrive, she simply jumps in the bathtub and dunks her hair. She then spends the next three hours fixing her hair to be presentable. Marwa is more straightforward. She simply comes out, meets the boy, looks straight at him, and asks him something like, "Do you think Kierkegaard meant we can only resolve the mind-body dichotomy through faith, and faith alone, which would mean Schopenhauer was wrong, or do you think he meant there is no resolution, or do you think he was ignorant to even ask the question, since Kant says there is no dichotomy, it is all an illusion?" The mother wraps her boy, even if he does have an erection, and takes him home.

The girls are part of the war generation. They left Lebanon and saw the world. Would they be able to make the adjustments or would the country accommodate them? They both dated while they were here, but neither would consider it serious. They were never able to completely shed their indigenous relationship with their culture.

They are a new breed, a new species. I remember Kurt asking them a couple of years ago whose suffering was greater—Marwa's, whose family was shattered at an early age, or Nawal's, who experienced it later. They looked at Kurt as if he were completely nuts.

———

I just read the peace plan in Lebanon between Hizballah and Israel. It sounds like a tag team professional wrestling match with too many referees.

———

A paleographic document was unearthed from the ruins of downtown Beirut. Dr. Ullano Signori, an orthographer from Bari, was finally able to decipher it. The message read:

The truth is that we all live by leaving behind; no doubt we all profoundly know that we are immortal and that sooner or later every man will do all things and know everything.

That was followed by an indecipherable paragraph. It was written in a language unknown to man. Dr. Signori suggested that it was the author's intent to obfuscate the message.

The last paragraph read as follows:

What one man does is something done, in some measure, by all men. For that reason a disobedience done in a garden contaminates the human race; for that reason it is not unjust that the crucifixion of a single Jew suffices to save it. Perhaps Schopenhauer is right: I am all others, any man is all men.

Dr. Signori was flabbergasted when he deciphered the title of the document. It was called *Ficciones.* He wondered what an Argentine was doing in Phoenicia.

————

The war started. No one was sure what was going to happen. My parents kept discussing whether I should leave and study abroad. Karim left for Washington, DC. That is where I was born. He enrolled at George Washington University. I missed him already.

I stayed in Beirut till I graduated from high school. The war made everything very difficult. I went to university in France. It was there I reestablished contact with Karim.

I was living in a flat with four other guys, all French. One day, he just appeared at my door. He was in Paris on the way to Beirut for Easter break. It was as if we had never parted. If we were close at one time, we were now even closer, for the age difference was no longer significant. He was still as handsome as ever. He was there for only a day, so we spent the whole time just catching up. That night, he spent it with me, in my own bed. We did not have sex, of course, as I was still too afraid to tell anybody. I was definitely terrified of telling him anything. That night, we got high again, in our underwear, and he played guitar just for me.

I went to visit him the following year. I spent a week with him. I stayed at his apartment, of course, and spent the nights in his bed. Even though it was my hometown, so to speak, he played the perfect host. He still had not graduated. I didn't think he really ever wanted to. He was having a wild time. He owned a motorcycle. He was very popular with the girls, and made sure to show me all his past conquests.

During that week, we took the shuttle to New York City. I had never been to New York. I wanted to see everything. He wanted to fuck a prostitute. He called a whorehouse he had heard of. We went there. He picked the sexiest hooker and I had to settle for one that was barely passable. An hour later he was bragging he came three times. I admitted I came only once. I did not admit I barely came once. There was a knock on the door when my hour had passed, and the prostitute asked me if I was sure I wanted to come. The poor thing must have had lockjaw. She had been sucking my dick for an hour and I did not come. I finally masturbated myself to orgasm.

On the way back to DC in the evening, the stewardess was infatuated with Karim. She told him he looked like Rex Reed, except his eyes were prettier. She slipped him her phone number.

I did not see him again for another eighteen months. I went back to DC to check out Georgetown University. That was where I wanted to get my graduate degree. I stayed with him for another week. I was more in love with him than ever. He considered me his closest friend. We spent many a night in his bed. He did not want to have sex with his girlfriend at the time because she refused to have sex with both of us at the same time. He said we would move in together if I went to school there.

One night still sticks in my memory. I woke up when I felt him hugging me. He had his arms around me, his chest snuggling to my back, and his erection plastered on my butt. Only our briefs stood in the way. He was sleeping soundly. I had the courage to actually put my hand between us and touch his erection. He rolled back over to his side of the bed. I took his hand and held it in mine. I loved him so much. He woke up. I pretended to be asleep.

The next day, he asked me if I realized at one point during the night, I had held his hand. I told him I had not realized that. He dropped the subject.

I was accepted at Georgetown. I called him to tell him I was coming over. I had decided to tell him everything. We were going to be living in the same town, most probably in the same apartment. I was going to tell him I was gay. I was going to tell him I was in love with him, had been since the day I met him. I felt more confident. I was coming out of the closet.

He never returned my call.

I got a call from my mother. She said she had some bad news. She said my friend Karim died in a motorcycle accident. He was so drunk he actually drove right into a wall.

I was devastated.

About a year later, I had a man in my apartment in DC. We were lying in bed together, after a fairly dull sexual assignation. He happened to look at my nightstand and notice a picture of Karim.

"He was a handsome man," he said. "Was he a lover?"
I told him he was my best friend.

"It was sad how he died, wasn't it?"

"Did you know him?" I asked incredulously.

"Not really. He just hung around the Spike. He never went home with anybody. Nobody I know of ever had sex with him. He just hung around and got drunk."

"He hung around a gay bar?" My voice betrayed me.

"Oh yeah. He got drunk at the Spike the night he died. We all saw him hit the wall."

———

I pine for pine. That is a funny way of putting it, but I really do miss the smell of pine. There are various trees back home, each with its own charm, yet it is the pine trees I miss. Specifically, I miss the scent of pine trees. And, contrary to what most Americans assume, they do not smell like house-cleaning detergents. I do miss the olive trees, and I do miss the oaks. I also miss the cedars. However, it is the smell of pine that gets me. It calls me home.

I pine for pine.

———

Oh, my heart, do not rise up to bear witness against me!

This is an inscription from the Book of the Dead. It's good, isn't it?

———

An hour later. Arjuna and his charioteer, Krsna, on the battlefield. They are now joined by Eleanor Roosevelt, Krishnamurti, Julio Cortázar, and Tom Cruise, who looks a little lost.

ARJUNA: Why me?

KRSNA: What do you mean?

ARJUNA: Why me? Why do all things have to happen to me?

KRSNA: Oy vey.

KRISHNAMURTI: Is he still singing the same tune?

ELEANOR: He's been like this for the last half hour.

ARJUNA: Go ahead. Make fun of me. Go ahead. You all think you are so smart and know everything. I just want to understand.

JULIO: What's there to understand? I told you, understanding is an intellectual requirement, nothing more.

ELEANOR: Go out and kill your cousins.

KRSNA: Stop trying to make sense out of everything. Nothing makes sense.

TOM: Why me?

ELEANOR: Oh, shut up.

ARJUNA: Why me, O God, why me?

KRSNA: Because you are a soldier.

It was humid, a sweltering day. She was beginning to regret her decision. The taxi had moved barely a hundred meters in the last half hour. She was perspiring profusely. It was going to be an unusually bad summer. They would probably have to go up to the mountains sooner than they thought.

She wondered if she should turn back. They would understand if she did not make it. She had only said she would try. "Why don't you come over for lunch tomorrow?" Marie-Christine had said. "There will be so many people you haven't seen in years. It would be like the good old days."

There were so many people crossing. She wondered who all these people were. Traffic was backed up in both directions. Some were obviously going to work, some were probably visiting friends. So many people.

Crossing the infamous Green Line.

She was born thirty years ago, on the other side, in Furn Ishibek. There were no sides then, of course. One city, her city, Beirut. She was a true Beiruti. Even though many people were born and raised in Beirut, they were not Beirutis. To be one, you had to be from a family who had always been one. One would be able to tell from the name where someone was from, which city or village, even if that person had never been to that village. That was where his family was from, that was where he was from. She was not married to a Beiruti though. He was from the South. In her blood, no matter what others say, she is still Beiruti.

Crossing from West to East.

She paid the cab. She had to get out at the barricade. She stood in line waiting to present her paper to the Syrian agent who manned the checkpoint. It was a long line. It was humid. She felt the stares.

She had worried all the night before, wondering what to wear. She knew she would have to walk, but she still wanted to make a good impression. She decided on a light Lacroix dress to accommodate the heat. She realized it was the wrong choice. The dress made her more attractive. The heels were not a good idea, either.

"Identity card," the Syrian blurted out loudly. He moved closer to her. She backed off a step and handed him her card. Like the Lebanese passport, those cards have a person's complete history: age, sex, religion, profession, marital status, etc. He scrutinized her card. If he turned her back, she would be relieved. Unlike the hundreds who were in line behind her, she was not exactly afraid of what a Syrian could do to her. Her husband's name was on her card, and even though this agent seemed to be another one of those uneducated rabble Syria produced in abundance, she was sure he would recognize the name.

"Why are you going to East Beirut?" he asked gruffly.
"To have lunch," she said.

He shook his head in disbelief and let her pass.

It is a long walk to the National Museum, or the military depot which was once the National Museum, where the barricade of the other side was. Maybe they would turn her back. The jacaranda trees surprised her, both because they had withstood all the fighting, whereas the surrounding buildings had not, and because they were bursting in blue-blossomed splendor. She walked, noting the complete destruction of the area. This was a beautiful section of Beirut at one time. In the old days, they would erect risers where the politicians and dignitaries stood saluting and viewing the troops on Independence Day. On her right was Beirut's famed race course. No horses ran these days. It was completely destroyed. She did not want to think about the museum itself. Everybody knew the treasures had been looted, but no one was quite sure who had done the looting. The pockmarked buildings on her left were unoccupied. Even the poorest refugees did not dare occupy them. This was the Green Line.

She felt all eyes on her. The line to get into East Beirut was forming. This was going to take some time. She was afraid. She should not have come. Everybody said it was completely safe, yet she was afraid. She did not trust the Christian militias.

"Identity card," the militiaman blurted out loudly. He moved closer to her. She backed off a step and handed him her card. He scrutinized her card. She felt someone scrutinizing her. She looked up, but did not see anybody. She looked farther. A fighter stood in front of his white Range Rover. He was smiling at her. She looked down, averting her eyes.

"Why are you going to East Beirut?" he asked gruffly.
"To visit a friend," she replied obsequiously.
"What's your friend's name?" His tone got softer.
"Marie-Christine Ashkar."
"Where are you from, madam?" He smiled.
"I'm a Beiruti."
"I am too. We are honored to have you visit us, madam. Welcome."

She was in. She thought it was easy. She should bring the boys next time. She would be able to show them the house she grew up in. She looked for the white Range Rover, but it was no longer there. She might make the lunch on time. She never did. Her problems started at the next checkpoint.

––––––

The good old days. My friends always talk about the good old days. You could fuck whomever you wanted. No condoms, no worries. The bathhouses were full, sex on the streets. It was liberating. No dating, no relationships, not even dinner. A quick blow job here, a quick fuck there.

I did not really know the good old days. People started dying when I came out.

The good old days. Everybody talks about the good old days. You could go anywhere you wanted without being afraid of being killed. No Israeli planes, no Syrian tanks, no shells waking you up at night. Snow skiing in Faraya, then down for a dip in the Mediterranean at Khaldé. No refugees in the Saint Simon beach club. You could actually walk the *trottoir* at Raouché. No kidnapping, no disappearances.

I did not really know the good old days. I was too young when the war started.

––––––

As for death, one gets used to it, even if it's only other people's death you get used to.

Enid Bagnold is a big fucking liar.

––––––

88

She got into the waiting taxi. At least the taxis on both sides look the same. They say East Beirut is much cleaner. She probably would not be able to tell until she got farther away from the barricade. Right now, it looked like the same city. She told the taxi where she wanted to go. She even told him exactly how she wanted to go there. This was her city.

The taxi stopped at the next checkpoint. The militiaman asked for her card. He scrutinized the card. He asked her to get out of the car. Instinctively, she asked if there was anything wrong. "No, ma'am," the youngster said. "We would just like to ask you a few questions." The taxi driver was visibly shaking.

She controlled herself as she got out of the car. Another militiaman led her towards a dilapidated building. She saw, out of the corner of her eye, the youngster telling the taxi driver to move on. She walked erect, holding her purse close. Just before she entered the building, she saw the white Range Rover.

On the second floor, she was led to the only room which still had a door. All the others, one could actually see into from the corridor due to shell damage. The militiaman knocked on the door softly. When the reply came, he opened the door, let her in, and closed it behind her.

He was sitting on a Louis XIV chaise lounge, watching her intently. He gestured for her to sit down on a low ottoman. She looked up at him.

"May I have your card, please?" he asked in French. She gave it to him. He pretended to scrutinize the card. "What are you doing in these parts, Mrs. Marchi?"
"I am going to lunch at a friend's house."
"What is your friend's name?" he asked.

"Marie-Christine Ashkar."

"Ah, an interesting woman," he said. She was not sure what he meant by that remark. Was he using a prurient tone? He was smiling. She was nervous.

"This is the first time you've come to East Beirut, isn't it?"

"I was born here." Defiance.

"But you are no longer from here," he insisted. "It is your first time." He looked at her, still smiling. "Things have changed a great deal," he went on.

"I understand."

"You speak French very well. You could fit here real well."

"I am from here."

"Why did you marry that fat faggot?" he asked suddenly.

"I beg your pardon." She tried not to show her shock.

"You heard me. Why did you marry that fat faggot?" He was still smiling, laughing almost.

"I will not sit here and be insulted." Indignation.

"Yes, you will," he said joyfully. He was having a good time. "I am not insulting you. I am insulting your husband."

"I don't know behind which herd you were raised, but in a civilized community, when you insult a woman's husband, you insult the woman."

"It's a different world, Samia."

"Don't call me by my first name. You have no right."

"I have every right, Samia. I can do whatever I want. I am the one who gives rights in this part of town." He said it all in a good-natured manner, as parent lecturing a favorite child. She was terrified. She controlled herself. His eyes asked her to join in the fun.

"Now, back to my original question," he continued. "Why did you marry that fat faggot? I really would like to know."

"He is not a homosexual," she insisted. He finally roared with laughter.

"That's right," he joked. "They bring him the boys every night, and he plays Chinese checkers with them." His brown eyes twinkled continuously with eager affability.

"There are no boys. I don't know what you are talking about."

He moved closer. "Your driver, Jihad, brings him a boy every Monday, Wednesday, and Friday night at six P.M. like clockwork." He was looking intently at her. "Did you know about that?"

"No," she replied. She was still controlling herself. "It's not true. Where would Jihad bring the boys to? He can't take them to the office."

"He has an apartment at Ramlel Baida. Much better than the one you live in. I can show you photographs if you want."

"You have photographs of my husband having sex with boys?" He roared with laughter again.

"I wish. Those would be fun to look at. No, I have pictures of the boys getting into the apartment building. They are all under seventeen, in case you're interested."

"Then you can't prove anything. They are just rumors. They are just old rumors."

"Samia, look at me," he said gently. "Your husband fucks little boys. Not only that, he provides young boys for his friends to fuck as well. He has been doing that for twenty years. Who do you think brought all the boys to Arafat all those years back? Why do you think the Syrian brass like him so much?"

"That is just a rumor."

"Okay. Okay. You still haven't answered my question. Why did you marry that fat . . . prick? How many years older is he? Thirty?"

"Twenty-six. And it is none of your business. Obviously you think you know more about my marriage than I do. Make up your own answers."

"It can't be the money. Your family is rich. It can't be connections. Twelve years ago, he was nothing but a small-time pimp. We know it can't be the sex. What would make a beautiful eighteen-year-old marry a fucking asshole like Marchi?"

She pulled her purse and stood up. "It is none of your fucking business," she said angrily. "I want to go home. You can kill me now, otherwise I am just walking out of here and going home."

He was smiling again. "I'll have a driver take you. He could drop you at your house. He'll cross over at the Franciscaine."

"No, thank you. I would rather walk."

"No, you would not," he laughed. "My driver will take you. He can get you to your house in fifteen minutes. It's much easier."

"Fine. Fine. I just want to get out of here."

"I want to see you again."

"What?"

"I want to see you again." He was standing beside her at the door.

"You are sick," she said. "You are very sick. I would rather die. You are very sick."

"I assume your husband is not having sex with you—"

"You are a sick man," she interrupted him. "I want to get out of here."

"But if he does touch you again, I will personally cross over and kill him myself."

"You are a sick man."

"My name is Nicola Akra, by the way, but you can call me Nick." He smiled.

The heat was stifling as she left the building.

Subject: Charges against Nicole Ballan

BEIRUT, Lebanon—A lawsuit against the former beauty queen and her boyfriend was filed by the State Prosecutor. The couple are charged with filming a homemade porno movie. Two other men are charged as well with the distribution of the film. If found guilty of making the film with the intent of selling it, both parties face sentences of one year in jail.

Nicole is a beauty, one of those extraordinarily beautiful Lebanese girls. The boyfriend has such a big penis, even the straight men have no compunction talking about it. The film became the centerpiece of Lebanese conversation for a hell of a long time. A couple decides to give the public what they want and their lives are ruined in the process. Nicole had modeling contracts with a couple of French firms who withdrew their offers when the scandal erupted. She was also unable to get a visa to any European country. She is stuck in Lebanon. She opened a store in the Zouk, a northern suburb in Beirut, selling *abbayes*. Nobody wears *abbayes* much these days, and those that do wear them only as house robes, yet her small store has a line of men desperately trying to get in and buy something. They come from all over Lebanon. The men who ruined her life would pay anything to get a glimpse of her.

———

It is true. He is right.

"Nick is a great guy," the driver says cheerfully. If she keeps quiet, he'll probably stop talking. They keep getting younger. He, on the other hand, is probably the same age as she. She is sitting in the back seat of the Range Rover, the current car *du jour* of gangsters and militiamen. Her husband has one, of course.

There is nobody at the Franciscaine crossing, which takes its name from the Franciscan school. The car breezes past the Christian checkpoint. When it gets to the other checkpoint, the driver shows them a government pass and is let through. Mr. Akra must be important.

"I want you to relay a message to your boss," she says calmly.
"Yes, ma'am."
"Tell your boss that if he ever sets foot in this part of town, I will have him killed. Very slowly."
The driver is aghast. He did not expect that.
"Can you relay the message, exactly, or should I send it with somebody else?"
"I'm sorry, ma'am," he stutters. "But why? Nick is a great man. He is a gentleman too."
"You just give him the message, okay?"
"Yes, ma'am. Does that mean you don't like him?"
She shakes her head in disbelief. Her ten-year-old is smarter than this.
"He will be disappointed, ma'am. I think he likes you. He told me I am supposed to remember how to get to your house because I will be picking you up to help you cross over."
"He told you what?" The man is completely crazy. "Just give him the message. Just give him my message."

———

Sex. In America an obsession. In other parts of the world a fact.

Marlene Dietrich said that. She never used verbs because she was a cheap German.

———

I wake up in my own room. I try to get up. I am unable to. I can't move. There is nothing constraining me. I should be able to get up. I am unable to. I am terrified. I realize I am still sleeping. I am dreaming. I wake up. I try to get up. I am unable to. I can't move. There is nothing constraining me. I should be able to get up. I am unable to. I am terrified. I realize I am still sleeping. I am dreaming. I wake up. I try to get up. I am unable to. I can't move. There is nothing constraining me. I should be able to get up. I am unable to. I am terrified. I realize I am still sleeping. I am dreaming. I wake up. I try to get up. I am unable to. I can't move. There is nothing constraining me. I should be able to get up. I am unable to. I am terrified. I realize I am still sleeping. I am dreaming. Life is a repeating pattern.

———

Brain stem, you say? By that definition, Juan should have been declared dead long before he even got to the hospital. I went to visit him and I could not believe what I saw. How do I describe the state he was in? He had his eyes open, but he was unconscious. Insensate? Insentient? But he wasn't catatonic. He was shaking constantly. Palsied? He was drooling continuously, farting every ten seconds.

His lover told me I could speak to Juan. He could hear me. Speak to him? I wanted to shoot him and put him out of his misery. He had completely lost motor coordination.

God is merciless. Juan had claimed he beat the virus. He went around the country lecturing on how he overcame AIDS. He felt better. Bang. What a way to go, huh?

I wonder if he was conscious. Just think of it. What if it were you? You are lying in a hospital bed. Spittle oozing out of your mouth constantly. You have to rely on your loved ones to wipe it for you, but it is endless, so they stop doing it. You are constantly shaking, not mild shaking, but heavy shaking, like an epileptic seizure. Think about this. All your loved ones are there and you keep farting every ten seconds. You can't stop. Fart, fart, fart, fart, fart. How would you feel? It's a good thing you have not eaten anything in a while. Who knows what would come out of your butt then?

Don't worry. It won't happen to you.

––––––

Firing on Israel has a long history. The PLO started it. Before the war, the PLO basically occupied southern Lebanon. The Lebanese government was powerless to stop them. The PLO even collected taxes from the Lebanese farmers, who were mostly Shiites. Just as they did with Hamas, the Israelis started helping the Shiites in the south organize and defend against the PLO. Those Shiites later became Hizballah.

The Shiites fought the PLO, but when the Israelis invaded in 1982, they turned their attention to their new enemy, Israel. The Israelis then started helping the Christians in the South organize and defend against Hizballah. Those Christians became the South Lebanese Army.

Hizballah learned much from the PLO, but they introduced a few sadistic twists of their own. What they did learn, though, was how to fire rockets across the border into Israel. They used the well-known military tactic of fire and run, which is sometimes called, by those in the know, the *Ya Rabbi Tegi Fi Aino* school of advanced warfare. *Ya Rabbi Tegi Fi Aino* is an Egyptian virus, first discovered in June of 1967, probably in the Sinai. It afflicts Semites in the Middle East, both Arabs and Israelis. Those infected with the virus are known to close their eyes, and fire, hoping to hit something. Translated from the Egyptian dialect, *Ya Rabbi Tegi Fi Aino* means "Oh God, I hope this gets him in the eye."

Hizballah would fire rockets into northern Israel, hoping to hit something. They actually begin running away before the rockets hit anything. If a rocket lands in Israel and not southern Lebanon, they declare victory. If it actually hits something, like some poor sucker's house, they declare complete victory. This is not an uncommon tactic among Arabs. Assad is called the Hero of October by the Syrians, based on his performance in the October war of 1973. You would think losing that war would not make one a hero, but he did give the Israelis a scare, attacking them on Yom Kippur, so he is the Hero of October.

The Israelis fire back. They use heavier weapons, but they too are afflicted with the *Ya Rabbi Tegi Fi Aino* virus. They hit everything but Hizballah targets. In all their attacks, not one Hizballah fighter has fallen, not one Hizballah target. They have, however, killed many southern boys who might have one day grown up to be Hizballah fighters, so it evens out in the end.

So there you have it, a brief history of the Middle East version of *The Art of War*. Who needs poor old Sun?

Death comes in many shapes and sizes, but it always comes. No one escapes the little tag on the big toe.

The four horsemen approach.

The rider on the red horse says, "This good and faithful servant is ready. He knoweth war."

The rider on the black horse says, "This good and faithful servant is ready. He knoweth plague."

The rider on the pale horse says, "This good and faithful servant is ready. He knoweth death."

All three together chant:

When the sun shall be darkened,
When the stars shall be thrown down,
When the mountains shall be set moving,
When the pregnant camels shall be neglected,
When the savage beasts shall be mustered,
When the seas shall be set boiling,
When the souls shall be coupled,
When the buried infant shall be asked for what sin she was
     slain,
When the scrolls shall be unrolled,
When the heaven shall be stripped off,
When Hell shall be set blazing,
When Paradise shall be brought nigh,
Then shall a soul know what it has produced.

"What the hell is this?" the rider on the white horse asks. "Those are not my words. I never said that. You guys are reading from the wrong fucking book, you idiots. That's the Qur'an. You're not allowed to read from that when you're with me. The Bible is my book. What the fuck am I supposed to do with you guys? Pregnant camels? Pregnant camels? We're in America now. Who cares about stupid camels anyway?"

The cantankerous rider on the white horse leads the other three lemmings away.

I would give anything for a good night's sleep.

———

If I had my life over again, I would form the habit of nightly composing myself to thoughts of death. I would practice the remembrance of death. There is no other practice which so intensifies life. Death, when it approaches, ought not to take one by surprise. It should be part of the full expectancy of life. Without an ever-present sense of death, life is insipid. You might as well live on the whites of eggs. You might as well drink Kool-Aid.

Muriel Spark wrote that. Then again, she probably didn't. I did. I may have read it in *Memento Mori*. How could I, though? She is British. They don't have Kool-Aid. I wrote that, not poor deluded Muriel.

How would you like to go through life with a name like Muriel?

———

Mohammad had a show in DC in 1988. Like most Lebanese, I had heard of him, but had never seen his work. I had met his sister,

Nawal, once, though. I really did not know what to expect, having never followed modern art. Most paintings in contemporary museums completely baffled me; the sculptures and installations, I would have thrown out with my garbage. Artistically, I have been indoctrinated in Lebanon. The art movements reached their peak with the Impressionists and have been on a quick decline ever since. Give me Monet or give me death.

I went to the opening reception with my lover, Mark. He was much more up-to-date on modern painting. It was crowded. We could not see all the paintings at once because of all the people. Mark led me to one of the paintings. We stood in front of it. It was stunning. I did not want to move. I kept looking at it for a couple of minutes, when an effeminate young man came and stood beside us.

"It's a beauty, isn't it?"
"Yes," I replied.

He told us his name. Jack, I think it was. He was with the gallery. I liked him. Unlike most salesmen, he made no bones about the fact he was trying to sell us a painting. He said Mohammad's paintings were already in some of the best collections in the country. They had just sold a painting to a museum, but he couldn't tell us which one. We had never asked. I told him I would love to have the painting, but I probably could not afford it. I asked about the price. He quoted an exorbitant sum. It was more than our annual income before taxes. We laughed together. I did like him. He admitted he was still new at the job. We talked some more about the paintings.

"I love his abstractions more than his realistic paintings," he said.
"I have never seen his abstract paintings," I said.

Both Mark and Jack looked at me strangely.

"These are abstract paintings, dear," Mark said.

"Oh, really?" I was embarrassed. I really did not know much about art. "I thought if you could tell what they are, they are not abstract."

"Can you tell what these are?" Mark asked. "They are all just paintings with irregular rectangles."

"Oh sure, but they are sides of our houses. That's what they look like in our villages. He painted them beautifully. I can see the stones clearly. That's how the stones look back home. Exactly that yellow color. All the other color highlights in each painting are different because of light conditions."

Jack excused himself, saying he should get the director to talk to us. I sounded like an expert. I thought it was clear as day. That is why I found the paintings beautiful. They were of my home village. They were of every village, Druze, Christian, or Muslim. He had captured Lebanon. They were so beautiful. Mohammad, by placing these large paintings around the gallery, had turned the place into a Lebanese village. Finally, someone was telling the tale of my home. He did not skip over it.

We heard the sound of raucous laughter. Mohammad walked over to us, accompanied by Jack and another man, probably the director. I recognized Mohammad right away. He was what we would call cursed. He was dark, looked like an Arab. In Lebanon, that's a curse. He had a beard and his hair was disheveled. He had a smile that was contagious.

"You had to ruin it, didn't you?" he said in Arabic.

"I'm sorry. I didn't know."

"Don't worry about it. I thought everybody would see what the paintings were when they saw them. Nobody did, so I didn't tell them. Makes you wonder about these Americans."

He shook my hand. "Mohammad," he said. No last name. "Samir Bashar," I said. "And this is . . ." I wanted to say lover. I did not know how in Arabic. His eyes understood. *"Habibi* is close enough," he said smiling. "This is my lover, Mark." I said it in French.

"If you had told me what these paintings were about," the director interrupted, "I would have promoted the exhibit completely differently."

"Put one of your dots on this painting," Mohammad told the director. "I want them to have it."

"But . . ." The director was stuttering.

"I'll send you the painting you liked last year. You can sell that one."

"Wonderful." The director placed a red dot sticker next to the painting.

"You can come pick this painting up when the show is over," Mohammad told me.

"I can't," I argued. "This is very generous, but we can't take it." I could see the look of pure delight on Mark's face. I was glad he couldn't understand what I was saying.

"I will hear none of it," Mohammad said. "This is now your painting." Tradition, and manners, required I refuse it twice more. It was so beautiful.

"I can't take this," I said. "This is too much. We don't deserve it."

"Nonsense. I wouldn't have it any other way."

"This is too much."

"Do not disgrace me by refusing my gift."

"Thank you so much," I said. "I will place it in the most honored place in my house. How long are you staying in DC? You must honor us by coming to dinner. How about tomorrow night?"

"You really don't have to," he said.

"We would love to have you for dinner." He had to give me one more chance to renege.

"I don't want to impose."

"I insist."

"That would be wonderful. Tomorrow it is."

It is ingrained.

———

Death is an endless night so awful to contemplate that it can make us love life and value it with such passion that it may be the ultimate cause of all joy and all art.

Paul Theroux was inebriated, peeing in the fireplace, when he said that. After reading one of his books, you can tell he hasn't contemplated death. Am I right, or what?

No, Jackson Pollock was peeing in the fireplace. Paul Theroux wrote books.

———

Scott said he wanted to be immortal. He wanted to be cremated. He wanted me to use his ashes in a painting.

I was unable to do it for a long time. I had always made my own paints, so the technical aspect of his request was not difficult. I could not bring myself to do it. I tried to convince myself that I had done my part in his immortality project. I had painted five portraits of him, one of which was already in a major collection.

It was midnight when I started the painting. I ground the ashes in linseed oil. I laid down a black ground. I painted a lotus blossom with the ashes in the center, and nothing else on the painting. It was a muddy painting because of the medium, but I made sure the blossom was beautifully drawn.

It became the centerpiece of my own collection.

———

June 17th, 1996
Dear Diary,

I am not sure I can stand this city anymore. If I never see another cellular phone for the rest of my life, it would be too soon. Everybody has one and everybody uses them all the time. It is so irritating. We went to a restaurant tonight and phones just kept ringing. Every table averaged about three phones. Not a minute went by without one phone ringing. The ringers are all set to weird songs. You are nobody if you don't own a cellular. I refuse to touch one. I heard a fight erupted at the Rabelais two nights ago and the men started hitting each other with their cellular phones. One man needed seven stitches over one eye.

———

Fatima felt something bad was about to happen. It was a feeling in her bones. Today was going to be a bad day. April 13, 1975. She wished it was over. She rode the bus with other Palestinians that day. She wanted to get home and lock herself in.

She heard on the news that an unsuccessful attempt was made on the life of Pierre Gemayel a couple of hours before. She knew that meant trouble. She didn't like the man because of his constant antagonistic rhetoric, but she did not wish him dead. He was a troublemaker. Gemayel was a Maronite leader and founder of the Phalangist Party, which had its own militia. It was going to be trouble.

The bus was passing through Ain El Rummanneh when it was stopped. She looked out the window and saw men with guns, wearing sacks with eye holes. She started shaking. They asked everybody to get out of the bus. She followed. The armed men lined the passengers along the bus. She noticed some passersby stopped to figure out what was happening. One of the masked men fired a warning shot in the air and the street emptied. One of the armed men asked if there was anybody on the bus who was not Palestinian. A passenger said his mother was Lebanese. The man with the sack shot him in the head at point-black range, calling his mother a whore.

She was getting hysterical. She lost count of how many people they had killed by the time the gunman came to her. She was on her knees. She begged for mercy. The sack asked her if she had any children. "Not yet," she sobbed. She wanted to beg some more, but he interrupted her. "Well, we can't have you producing more assholes now, can we?"

He shot her.

Twenty-eight Palestinians were killed on that bus.

The war has started. Buckle up. It is going to be a bumpy ride.

———

By the fireplace, on a calm and lonely night, Julio and I sat drinking *mate*. Our love of *mate* was one of the many things we had in common, since both Lebanese and Argentineans drank it. Another thing we both had in common was neither one of us could write very well. But what the hell, we sure could talk when we wanted to.

"Why have we had to invent Eden, to live submerged in the nostalgia of a lost paradise, to make up utopias?" Cortázar asked me. I realized he was depressed as usual. He never seemed to be able to pull himself out of it. I held back my first impulse to scream, "Snap out of it!" I had to calm down, create a moment of calm in response to his latest crisis.

"We create Eden to recreate the only moment of calm we really ever knew," I said wisely. "Life is hard, crazy. We long for the nine months of calm. We want to be back in the womb."

I realized I hit a nerve. Julio's left eye was nervously fluttering again. So many ticks, this man had.

"Reason is only good to mummify reality in moments of calm or analyze its future storms, never to resolve a crisis of the moment."

It was a good thing nobody was recording our conversation. I am not sure Julio would appreciate others finding out how he behaved when he was around me, how his mind worked in my presence. A disinterested observer might think the last sentence he uttered came out of the blue. He said it, however, because he knew I could follow his mind's inner working better than he could. I knew what he was about to say and was completely ready for him.

"You're having another crisis, Julio," I said. "Did you take your medicine today?"

"And these crises that most people think of as terrible, as absurd, I personally think they serve to show us the real absurdity, the absurdity of an ordered and calm world. But does anybody see this? No, they want Atlantis."

"It's a good thing a mother's vagina contracts after delivery or everybody would try to crawl back in," I told him calmly. "And then we grow, and the option is no longer available to us, yet we desperately yearn for it even more. You should write a story titled 'Return to Uterus the Great.' "

"Precisely, old man," he was now rambling. "What is war or disease, if not a revolt against a calm and ordered world, if not an example of the horror of a calm and ordered world? Would you rather have a world of AIDS or a world of fifties sitcoms? Those are your options. But does anybody listen? Life lives for itself, whether we like it or not."

I had an evil grin on my face when I told him, "Clarity is an intellectual requirement, nothing more. You insist that dialectics can only set our closet in order in moments of calm, yet here you are, trying to create a moment of calm, a moment of clarity in your current crisis, by using the only thing you know, dialectics."

I saw the reaction in his eyes. They looked at me, grasped the genius of what I said, tried to make sense of it, got this glazed look, and then his mind froze, just like a computer screen when it has too much information. His head tilted. He was out like a light.

Poor Julio. I try not to do this to him, but he's just too easy.

———

Joe and Christopher celebrated their seventeenth anniversary, in the presence of friends, by exchanging their IV lines. That celebration was the first time I met them. I was invited by Joe. They had bought a couple of my paintings years ago. Joe wrote me, suggesting my presence would be a delightful surprise to his partner.

I was welcomed into their lives at the eleventh hour. They both died within three months of that delectable night.

I arrived at their house sometime later to find Christopher sleeping, and Joe in a foul mood. I tried to figure out what had happened, but did not understand much of what he was saying. All I gathered was the fact Christopher had attempted to reopen the lines of communications with his estranged family. The entire family were devout Christians and it was causing problems. Joe was unable to elaborate more, something to do with a calamari soft-shell taco. I was bewildered.

He showed me a letter he had just finished typing to his brother-in-law. It elucidated the situation, but not by much:

———

Dennis.

I thought about calling and decided faxing you would be a better way to let you know what I want to tell you about your call to Christopher yesterday. I don't know if you realized it, but your call was greatly distressing to Christopher. I want you to know this will *not* happen again. It will not happen again because I will not allow it to happen again.

You may not realize it, but Christopher is dying. For someone who has seen him every day for the last sixteen years, this is very apparent. For someone who has seen him only once or twice, it may not be so. Christopher is very vulnerable and also very polite. He listened to what you had to say yesterday. I am not so vulnerable and also not so polite. The kind of call you made to him yesterday will not be tolerated. I will not have you calling here and upsetting him.

Let me make a couple of things very clear. Neither Christopher, nor I, are here to be your HIV or AIDS education service. If you had questions about the safety of Janice or Jennifer eating a taco that Christopher had eaten from, you could and should have called your local AIDS Hotline or the CDC Hotline. Knowing the facts about AIDS is your responsibility. Janice and Jennifer are adults. If they had any reservations about eating the taco, they could have simply said, "No thanks," or asked if it was safe.

Christopher was very hurt that you would even suggest that he would knowingly or unknowingly transmit HIV or put Janice or Jennifer in danger. This suggestion was insensitive, ignorant, and bigoted. What you said was very hurtful and harmful. You should consider what you say before you let something as ugly as that out of your mouth.

Your use (when you were here and over the phone) of the term *lifestyle choice* is offensive to both of us. We no more chose to be gay than you chose to be nongay. Why would anyone choose to be something so despised? Tell me why I would choose to be spit on and hit by strangers in the street for this "lifestyle." You may not care, but this has happened to me for being who I am and for happening to be on a public street.

Finally, you are not welcome to call or come to this house until you apologize to Christopher in writing. I will not let you do this to him again. If I find out that anyone tells Christopher about this letter (be that Janice or anyone else in his family), you will have no further contact with us. Christopher's time is too precious for him to be upset by your foolishness.

If you want to discuss this, you may call me on my private line at 415-555-2339.

Joe.

———

It was Christopher who later explained the situation. Janice, his sister, had come to visit him with her daughter, Jennifer. They ordered lunch from a gourmet Mexican restaurant. Christopher ordered calamari soft-shell tacos, which he thought were simply divine. He suggested that his sister and niece have a bite out of his taco, which they did. When Janice arrived home, she told her husband, who freaked. He phoned Christopher and accused him of being a killer.

While Joe fumed, Christopher kept repeating, "You should have tasted the tacos. They were fabulous."

Christopher lay dying when I saw them next. Joe showed me a letter from Christopher's stepfather, Al. Joe had previously asked him not to write Christopher anymore. Al swore, on the Bible, that he would never write them again. He lied.

———

Dear Christopher,

We're very sorry to hear that your not doing well. I felt a need to take the time to write to let you know we love you & are praying for you daily.

More than that God loves you and Joe, more than we could ever love you. In His book He tells us that "As sheep without a shepard we tend to go our own way & we suffer the consequinces of our sin. He also tells us that "We all have sinned and fall short of the glory of God." In another verse He tells us, "For the wages of sin is death, but the gift of God is eternal life in Christ Jesus our Lord."

No matter how we've lived or what we've done He waits with open arms to receive us. In first John 1:9 He says if we confess our sins, He is faithful and righteous to forgive us our sins & to cleanse us from all unrighteousness."

It would be wonderful to know that sometime in the future, we would meet on the other side, both you & Joe.

The both of you will always be in our prayers. My God reveal as to His presents & He is waiting with open arms.

Love, your mother & I, Al

———

I was furious. The letter got my blood boiling. My first reaction was to correct the spelling and grammar. I wanted to edit for punctuation.

I was on a nude beach on Maui once when three locals showed up. They were drunk, looking for trouble. They insulted everyone, men, women, gay or straight. They accused us of desecrating their island. They prodded the nudists, trying to instigate a fight, but none bit. Everybody started getting dressed and leaving. My companion started dressing. He wanted to leave. They came over while we were departing, and began insulting us. I was not offended by their insults. I was offended that I was being insulted by people who used incorrect grammar. I started correcting their English. I corrected their grammar, told them when they were repeating themselves, and reminded them that "we be real Hawaiians" and "youse gay people be bringing AIDS to the islands" were not proper English. My companion thought I was crazy, but the idiots were completely oblivious. They just went on and on until we got to the car and left.

I wanted to reply to Al's letter, but Joe would have none of it. After Christopher died, Joe sent his parents a letter telling him both he and Christopher had converted to Islam. As Mohammadans, God would be waiting for them with open arms, but with better presents.

Joe died not long after.

———

Out of timber so crooked as that from which man is made, nothing entirely straight can be carved.

Immanuel Kant said that, which I find so fascinating. He was also the first, to my knowledge, to postulate that time and space are created by man's mind. They do not exist without our perception, which is an interesting concept when you think about it.

I wonder if something entirely gay can be carved. That was a bad joke. I apologize.

Intuition and concepts constitute the elements of all our knowledge, so that neither concepts without intuition, nor intuition without concepts, can yield knowledge.

He said that too. When I was smarter, I had a reason for remembering those quotes together. I can't think anymore, however. I can't remember. It might have had something to do with time. Time is what I need right now, but the concept eludes me always.

———

I love you, Mohammad.
I love you, Scott.
I love you, Scott.
I love you, Kurt.
I love you, Mo.
I love you, Ben.
I love you, Mom.
I love you, Christopher.
I love you, Tim.
I love you, Kurt.
I love you, Joe.
I love you, Jim.
I love you, Alan.
Goodnight, John Boy.
I love you, Karim.
Hey, who said, "Goodnight, John Boy"?
I love you, Mr. Momad.
Isn't this *The Waltons*?
I love you, Kurt.
I love you, Juan.
Of course this isn't *The Waltons*.
I love you, Mahomet.
Where are we?
This looks like the last scene from *Longtime Companion*.
Don't say that. I hated that scene.
This isn't *Longtime Companion*.

This is the ending of a book.

Longtime Companion could have been called *The Waltons Do AIDS.*

You're sick.

Is this the last scene of a book?

I think they are trying to get a movie deal, which is why we need a sentimental ending.

I still love you anyway, Kurt.

This is stupid.

Is the book over?

I love myself the way I am.

We can't have the last scene without Steve.

This isn't the last scene.

Do you think this gratuitous sentimental scene is enough to clinch a movie deal?

I don't think this is as good as *Philadelphia.*

I was just wondering.

Philadelphia sucks. Tom Hanks is insipid.

Ask the reader. They have an objective view of this whole thing.

Okay. Hey you! Hey you! Do you think this is enough?

———

April 14th, 1989
Dear Diary,

Will it ever stop? Will it ever stop? How much longer can we suffer? How many more deaths before someone says enough?

Last night was one of the worst nights of the entire war. It was the worst. No one was able to sleep. The Syrians shelled the Christians, and the Christians bombed us. How could they do this? How can they keep going? Didn't they have enough?

The Syrians fired seven thousand shells into East Beirut.

Last night was the fourteenth anniversary of the beginning. A fitting celebration was held. Someone should bring the leaders together, put them in the same room, and kill them. How much more can we take?

———

A young woman opened the door. They hadn't told me someone else was going to be there.

"You must be Mohammad," she said in heavy accented English. Probably a recent arrival. "Come in."

She walked into the living room without introducing herself. I found myself having to hang my coat on my own. Samir's voice came from the kitchen. I was to come in and say hello. The kitchen smelled wonderful, just as I remembered. He was washing his hands, while his lover chopped tomatoes.

Samir came over and hugged me. "I'm sorry," was all he said. It was all he needed to say. We build our own family.

Mark made small talk. How was the trip? Did I know tabbouleh was difficult to make since they could never find real parsley? How was I handling life without Scott? Samir just watched me.

They kicked me out of the kitchen. They should be done in ten minutes.

I saw her sitting reading a magazine. She barely glanced up at me before going back to her reading. I sat down opposite her, not wanting to disturb her. I just wanted to look.

The lighting was perfect. It gave her black hair a warm highlight, making the cool shadows more vibrant. She wore a simple short black dress, a stark contrast to her skin. It was intense.

"It's not polite to stare," she said. She didn't stop reading.
"Nobody has ever accused me of being polite."
"Are you having some sort of heterosexual attack?" Heavy accent, but a definite command of the language.
"Don't flatter yourself. I'm only staring."

She put the magazine down, and smiled briefly at me. She lit a cigarette. She didn't ask if I minded.

"Okay. So what are you staring at?"
"I much preferred it when we weren't talking," I said.
"Fine by me." She picked up her magazine again. "Just remember that. For the whole two weeks, we aren't talking."
"What two weeks?" I asked. "I leave tomorrow."
"Funny. Funny. But I am not talking to you anymore."
Then it hit me. I was looking at my sister. Not the looks, but the mannerisms. This was Washington, DC. She behaved as if she knew me. I should have known.
"I'm sorry. I didn't know who you were."
"You mean you are rude to strangers as well."
I liked this girl.

Samir announced dinner. Marwa stood up, stuck her tongue out as she walked by.

"I see you two are getting along well." Samir chuckled.
"Marvelously," I said. "You should have told me she was coming to dinner."
"I didn't know," he said. "She just comes over whenever she feels

like it. We were neighbors while growing up, and we are now neighbors here."

"It must be fun," I joked.

"You'll get to experience it firsthand. I understand she will be staying with you guys for two weeks."

"I'm not sure I will be able to handle both of them."

"That's right," Marwa said, already seated at the table. "You're not only having a heterosexual attack. You're also having an incestuous one."

She was already serving herself. I liked this girl.

———

I wanted to write a book with Fabio on the cover. A stunningly beautiful American woman with perky breasts is sold as a slave to an Arab prince. He, on the other hand, is an incredibly successful American corporate executive pretending to be an Arab prince, for what American would fantasize about being seduced by an Arab.

Kidnapped and sold into slavery, the fiery Felicia Courtney realized that only her inexhaustible will could protect her honor. However, the nubile lass did not account for the sheer pulchritude and sex appeal of her ruthless master. His piercing emerald eyes saw through her soul, his muscular arms carried her into realms of unexplored passions. She found herself giving him her virginity willingly as the need to defy him melted away. She was his woman to do with as he pleased. Yet this perfect prince, who elicited her most intimate desires, was not what he seemed underneath his national robes. Blue-eyed Felicia could only hope their fires of passion would reveal his true secret identity. Their tempest of desires carried them beyond the harem walls into a mysterious Eden, where only magic and true love reside.

Then I realized I was copying the jacket of a book already published. There were hundreds of books with Fabio on the cover which had a Western woman kidnapped by an Arab who was really a Westerner in disguise.

I wanted to write an endless book of time. It would have no beginning and no end. It would not flow in order. The tenses would make no sense. A book whose first page is almost identical to the last, and all the pages in between are jumbled with an interminable story. A book which would make both Kant and Jung proud.

I was not able to do it. Besides, I would have been copying the master. Borges did it before me.

———

The first massacre of the war occurred in Karantina, in January, 1976. It did not affect me that much. In retaliation, the Palestinians and other leftist militias destroyed Damour, a Christian town. That one devastated me.

I did not know anybody killed in that bloodbath. It was not the gory pictures in the newspapers that baffled me. It was simply the concept. As a Druze, one would assume I would be more affected by the massacre at Karantina. I really had no idea where Karantina was, though. Damour, on the other hand, I passed through every day on my way to school. I loved that town. In one fell swoop, Damour no longer existed. They killed the people. Bloodied corpses, with open eyes, were left everywhere. Those who managed to escape on boats, left quickly, never to return. They hid in monasteries and convents in the mountains. The guerrillas stole everything. They ransacked the town, picked the houses clean. They took the clothes, silverware, tiles, doors, faucets, furniture, and even toilets. Then they burned the town and the surrounding citrus groves. Damour was no more. Expunged. Obliterated.

I never thought humans could do that.

———

What if there is no afterlife?

It does not exist, you know. You die. That's it. You cease to exist. No heaven. No hell. No reincarnation. No presents. No waiting for Judgment Day. You die. They bury you. They cremate you if you're lucky. That's it.

Kurt keeps trying to convince me an afterlife exists. His main argument is a simple one. If all religions, throughout the millennia, believed in an afterlife, there must be something there.

That argument is flawed, as any rational person would tell you. It does not even pass a simple Aristotelian test. Yet I hear it often, even from people I consider reasonably intelligent. The need for a belief in the nonfinality of death is so great it affects even usually logical people. I hope I do not have to elucidate all the rationales as to why all religions require an afterlife. "If there is no life after death," a Muslim theologian once told me, "the very belief in God becomes irrelevant, or even if one believes in God, that would be an unjust and indifferent God: having once created man and not concerned with his fate."

One of Kurt's favorite proofs for an existence of an afterlife is the Tunnel of Light. All those who have had a near-death experience have had practically the same vision. They see a tunnel with a bright light at the end, and deceased loved ones calling them or welcoming them into the light. That, for many, it seems, is conclusive proof an afterlife exists.

I always wondered why they all see loved ones. Where are the hated ones? In hell, I assume. Everyone you loved in your life will be there to meet you, all those you did not like very much are somewhere else. You, like Jesus, have that power. I would hope Rembrandt van Rijn is there to meet me. That would be more exciting. Gauguin would be in hell, since I loathe his paintings. Mondrian, yes, but not Malevich. Shakespeare, yes, but Chaucer should burn somewhere else. The Marxes, Karl, Groucho, Harpo, and Chico would be there, but not Zeppo. No dull people in my tunnel, thank you. This is fun, isn't it?

But what about the tunnel? What about the tunnel, you ask.

What about it? It isn't Nabokov's fountain after all. If you think about it, the one experience as stressful as death itself is birth. What does one see as one is being born? Possibly a tunnel, but I doubt welcoming loved ones. A slap on the butt is more like it.

I know, you say. You have proof. Many people remember past lives clearly. How is that possible, you ask.

Drugs is one possibility. Schizophrenia is another.

How come all people who remember their past lives were Cleopatra at some point? No one remembers being her maidservant, or the big shmuck with the big feather fan in the background, moving the fan up and down, up and down. Andy Rooney would wonder about that.

What if I told you matter creates consciousness? Would you believe me, or would you run away and hide behind your safe beliefs? You can call me a heresiarch, if it makes you feel better. I like that word.

Are you so afraid of this life? Are you still practicing, hoping to get it right in the next one? Are you being a good girl, hoping Father will reward you with everything you weren't able to get? Are you?

One day, you will write that book. One day, you will be fulfilled. Some day, you will take that risk. Some day soon, you will be doing what you really, really love. One day, you will begin to live your life.

What have you done with the garden entrusted you?

———

June 14th, 1993
Dear Diary,

I had a fascinating conversation with a Swiss woman today. She was visiting her sister who lives in Ashrafieh. It was good to see some of the Europeans coming back to Beirut. We talked about funerals and traditions in different cultures. She played the church organ every Sunday in Leysin. She said she had been playing there for over twenty-five years, and in all that time she had never seen a single person cry at a funeral, not one. This shocked the hell out of me. We both thought it was unnatural. So I tried to explain to her how at some of our funerals, we still have professional mourners. It doesn't happen as often these days, but some women are asked to come to funerals to mourn the dead person, eulogize, wail, all done loudly to make sure everyone cries. The mourners keep wailing until the loved ones have cried enough. It is shocking that in twenty-five years nobody has cried at a funeral in Switzerland. We are getting colder. We don't cry as much, but we aren't that cold yet. I find it hard to imagine.

———

Nabokov told me in an unguarded moment, "The cradle rocks above an abyss, and common sense tells us that our existence is but a brief crack of light between two eternities of darkness."

I was born in Beirut, the fifth son of my parents. I was the youngest child for the longest time. Nawal was born when I was twelve. Even after five sons, my father blamed my mother for having a girl. He was part of a generation that was supposed to have been extinct. He believed in continuing the legacy of his forefathers. He should have joined them.

My sister was a difficult birth. My mother did not recover easily. The doctors recommended an extended period of rest, which was patently impossible in our household. She continued to take care of the entire household for the next two years while she recuperated. I helped with my sister. For the first two years, I was my sister's nanny, diaper changer, baby-sitter, teacher, and all around play toy.

I left my family when I was fifteen, not knowing it was final. The war had started. I was sent to Los Angeles to be with my uncle and finish high school. I moved to San Francisco, attending the San Francisco Art Institute, in 1977. I could not afford to visit home during my college years. My father refused to help me financially to go to art school. I worked full time at various jobs to support myself, until my first show at Heller. After that show, I stopped having to worry about money or family. I gained financial independence and lost my roots.

My father came to visit me in Washington in the fall of 1983. I was nervous for three months prior to his arrival. I had to de-gay my apartment completely. It was not an arduous task, for I was not completely out of the closet then. Still, I worried endlessly. Cleaning out my books took the most time. I got a cardboard box to hide in my basement. In it, I placed Baldwin, Proust, Mishima, and Wilde. I even threw in Yourcenar's books just in case. Two days before he arrived, I panicked. I sent Nabokov's *Pale Fire* down as well. I did not wish to risk anything. Charles Kinbote could disinter me.

He tried to treat me like a man and I did not feel like one. He was proud of me and I felt I shamed him. He wanted us to be friends and I wanted him in Beirut.

I had never spent that much time alone with him. Hell, I do not think I had spent more than a couple of minutes alone with him my entire life.

Washington was his town. This was where he graduated from college. It was where he taught. It was where they conceived me. It was where he betrayed me.

I lived in a one bedroom. He asked me to disappear for a couple of hours. He wanted to recapture old times with an old flame. In my bed. Three times in the two weeks he spent with me. We were peers. I was a man now. I did not feel like one.

I wanted to understand. It was a different culture. He was a good man. My mother loved him. He loved my mother. Who was I to judge?

I judged.

Five years later, I was able to watch his face when I told him about the virus. His face contorted in pain when he finally believed me. I wanted him to rage. I could handle rage. I did not know how to handle pain.

I wanted him to rage, but I never did.

I told him I was a man now. I told him I was not like him. He sat there and cried. I had expected everything but that. I wanted to be in Washington, in my own bed.

I asked him once if he ever forgave me. He said there was nothing to forgive.

I wonder if he ever forgave me.

———

My country is being torn apart by packs of wild dogs, and my countrymen are apathetic.

———

Perhaps the whole root of our trouble, the human trouble, is that we will sacrifice all the beauty of our lives, will imprison ourselves in totems, taboos, crosses, blood sacrifices, steeples, mosques, races, armies, flags, nations, in order to deny the fact of death, which is the only fact we have.

Jimmy Baldwin wrote me that in one of his endless letters. I love the man, but he wrote really long letters. I wrote back, "Baldy boy [that was what I always called him], I loved the fact you wrote mosques instead of churches. I feel you are finally seeing the light."

———

Scott never wrote. He even hated writing letters. He was a reader. He enjoyed reading. It was his one true passion. He felt that if he ever wrote, he would lose the pleasure. He didn't want to risk it. I understood. I rarely enjoyed looking at painting.

———

East Beirut is Christian. West Beirut is mostly Muslim, but still fairly pluralistic. They have killed and kidnapped a number of Christians in West Beirut, but its nature remained more accepting of its heterogeneous population. They forcibly evicted all non-Christians out of East Beirut. They sanitized it. East Beirut is cleaner, tidier, more orderly, and antiseptic. They have no slums or refugee camps. They razed them.

If sterility is your cup of tea, then you would like East Beirut. It's like a smaller Marin County.

———

March 13th, 1995
Dear Diary,

Lamia Ghaleb came by to visit today and relayed a disturbing rumor. She had heard about a man in Beirut who had sex with his Filipino maid and got AIDS. He then gave it to his wife. His son also had sex with the maid and he got AIDS. Only the daughter in that family is uninfected. What a disaster. I hope it is not true.

Amin Bagdady was a hairdresser, a homosexual. He was by far the best in Beirut. His sexuality was rarely an issue with his clientele. It actually was rarely an issue with anybody. There were the jokes and whispers, but few made a big deal out of it. His family pretended to ignore it.

Being the best hairdresser, he was somewhat of a celebrity. His social life was pretty active because of that. The women who came to see him were the who's who of Beirut.

It was not until the Israeli siege of Beirut that he was truly loved. The Israelis had cut off the water and electricity. Most of his clients, but not all, had left the city. While the Israelis bombed the population, while everybody was terrified, wondering if they would be able to survive the onslaught, he kept his shop open. He had a small generator which provided power and he used cases of bottled water he had hoarded in preparation for just such an emergency. As the population of West Beirut ran thirsty, as they were walking around, unable to do laundry or shower, Amin's clients remained well coifed and well dyed. You could tell one of his clients from a distance simply by her hair. He became a hero.

Both he and his shop survived the Israeli bombing. He did not survive their withdrawal, however. He was murdered by Druze militiamen while visiting his relatives in his hometown, in one of the numerous massacres that occurred after the withdrawal.

Bashir Salaheddine
P.O. Box 892
Beirut, Lebanon

Mr. Samir Bashar,
920 29th Street NW
Washington, DC 20007

Dear Samir,

I apologize for the delay in answering your letter. In my old age, I do not like writing letters as much as I used to. It took me a while to gather my thoughts and find the courage to write you back.

I cannot tell you how happy I was to receive your note. Your mother brought it to me the day after she returned. Few members of the family are interested in our history. I have been patiently waiting for someone to ask me even a simple question. You were the first. So let me start by answering your questions before I delve into more personal matters.

You are right. Our families, both your father's and mother's, are descendants of the Tanoukh family. Most Druze families are descendants from the Tanoukhis, who were originally Arab tribes that migrated to Lebanon during the Abassid Dynasty to defend the coastal cities from Byzantine armies. You are right, as well, that they did rule part of Mount Lebanon for four hundred years, but they also ruled Beirut as well during that same period. During that time, they fought the Crusaders and the Turkmans. I believe this should fill some of the blanks in your research so far. Please do not hesitate to ask me any more questions. You do have to ask them quickly, though. Unlike our ancestor, Emir Salaheddine Amin bin Ghazy Al-Tanoukhi, who lived for a hundred and twelve vital years, I do not believe I will reach my centennial.

The questions you have raised in your note are justifiable. I am being presumptuous in telling you this, since, after all, you are the historian. However, I do feel having been educated in the United States may have distanced you from your actual subject. That could work to your advantage, as well as disadvantage. My education was in France (a long, long time ago!) which kept me in my environment for the most part. The reason you have found so many inaccuracies is easy for us to understand, although a little difficult for you. The manuscripts you are reading were written by narrators, not historians. Few people wrote about history in Lebanon. All of the writers who did were Christians, with a couple of exceptions. They were the only ones who were educated. In the sixteenth century, the Catholic Church helped the Christians open a school of theology in Rome. The monks of Lebanon studied there and returned to Lebanon to open schools in the mountains and teach theology. The Druze had no opportunity for education until the eighteenth century. From all the manuscripts you listed, all two hundred and thirty-two, only one was written by a Druze. There are others, of course, and I am attaching copies of everything I have to this letter. You do get the point, however. The Christian prejudice ran amok. They did some of the finest work in keeping records about Lebanon, but we need to be careful about considering them completely accurate.

I have to tell you how proud I am of the work you are doing. It was such a joy to receive your note and the research you have accomplished so far. I thought nobody in the family cared one way or another about our history. To find that someone was willing to put such an effort to bring forth our history brought joy to my heart. That the effort came from you was a double pleasure.

I do not have to tell you what uproar your last visit caused. Most of the family members have been unable to stop talking about it for the last couple of years. As you know, many refuse to have anything to do with you anymore. I was glad to find out at least your parents were somewhat understanding. I have received a number of calls chastising me for wanting to reply to your letter. For an old man like me, this has been a lot of fun, I can tell you!

I realize this might be a painful subject for you. I hope not. I hope you have adjusted to the way things are. Most of the members of the family, even those who shun you, are decent people. They just have never had to face someone with your courage. I do think it was courageous of you. I assume you know you are not the first. Your uncle was that way too. Of course, he died a bitter man. It was sad watching him suffer so much. I have been wondering how to say this, but I guess you have figured out by now where this is going. I, too, am a homosexual. I have been for the ninety-three years of my life. I just have not done anything about it. Unlike your uncle, I am not a bitter man. I married a wonderful woman and had a good life. I loved my wife very much and I still do my children. I did regret at times not having shared my bed with a man even once, but after a while, even those feelings dimmed. You do realize this is the first time I have ever told anybody, other than my departed wife, of course. At my age, I no longer care what others think.

I hope you can pardon the rambling of an old man. I needed to write what I did. As I said earlier, the fact that the request came from you, the one who is accused of ending the family line completely (You bad boy!), amuses me to no end.

I realize you may be facing some hard times, but keep your head up. You are a prince. You are Emir Samir Basil Bashar. I know that titles do not mean much anymore these days. Nonetheless, they should mean something to you. You are still a prince. God gave you that title.

I understand you are living with someone. I hope you two are happy together. I know it is practically impossible for you to bring him here when you next visit. I would have liked to meet him. Who knows? I am still in good health. Maybe I can arrange a trip to America at some point. It would be nice to visit you and meet your friend. I might be able to visit San Francisco. That has always been a dream of mine.

Please write again soon. The mail does work here sometimes. I did enjoy hearing from you. I hope this letter finds you in good health.

Sincerely,

Your great-great-uncle!
Bashir Salaheddine

———

I would have canceled the exhibit if I could. The gallery refused to even entertain the idea. Scott had just died, but the exhibit had been set for months. I flew to New York to set it up. I told the gallery I would be flying back the minute the exhibit was completely hung. I was not attending the opening reception.

As usual, we finished hanging the exhibit barely on time. It was only hours before the opening reception. I went to the hotel to pack. I ended up in the bar drinking. I was drunk when I decided to attend the reception and insult a few people.

I arrived while the reception was in full swing. I walked across the gallery to the open bar. I asked for a double Scotch on the rocks.

The director, Jana, asked me if I hadn't had enough. I waited till
I swallowed the whole thing before saying no.

I scanned the whole room. I saw my mother staring at me. I
laughed at myself. My mother was never this young. That reprov-
ing look was my mother's.

"Hey you," I scream across the room. "I painted you."
She walks towards me, sizing me up.
"Look," I tell Jana, pointing at one of the paintings. "I painted
her. I paint her all the time."
"You're drunk," the girl says softly. "You're making a fool of your-
self."
I am so confused. I can't reply. I haven't spoken in Arabic in so
long. I want to ask who she is. I know her. I know I know her. I
can't place her. I can't think straight anymore. She takes my hand.
"Come on," she says. "Let's go to my place. You can sleep it off."
I want to say something, but the language fails me. I struggle. The
words come out in Arabic.
"I killed him."
"Let's go home."
My sister leads me out by the hand. I weep.

————

She picked up the phone.

"Hello."
"I got your message."
"How did you get my number?"
"Come on, Samia. It's not that difficult to get what you want in
Beirut."
She composed herself.

"Don't call me here, please," she said. "I don't want to talk to you."

"Can I come see you?"

"No. What is the matter with you? I don't want to see you."

"But I do." he said. Still jovial, even on the phone.

"You are crazy. You know they would kill you if you cross."

"You think you would be able to hire someone?"

"I wouldn't have to. I found out who you are. There are a million people here who would love to get their hands on you."

"I love it," he laughed heartily. "You care about me."

"You're crazy. Absolutely nuts. I'm going to hang up now. Don't call me again."

She hung up the phone.

———

Death destroys a man: the idea of Death saves him.

The mild-mannered E. M. Forster said that. Eddy knew a thing or two.

———

There were only five of us who started the history doctoral program at Georgetown in 1983. By the second year, we were only four. We rarely hung out together socially. I was having a difficult time reintroducing myself to my countrymen. I left Washington when I was seven, came back when I was twenty-one. The change, in the city and in me, was palpable.

There was one girl in the program who intrigued me. She had an intellect far superior to mine. Her family was Catholic, blue blood from New England. Of course, she was loud, scruffy, obnoxious, and fun to be around. I probably was the only guy in the department she had not slept with. Her name was Wanda, but everybody called her Wicked.

January, 1984, was a hell of a cold month. I was leaving class and going home, when I heard her call my name. I saw her running at me, wearing a camel's hair coat, which made her seem twice her natural size. Her dark hair blowing in the brumal wind. She wore a long canary yellow scarf, Isadora Duncan–style, which was the only color I saw for miles around that bleak day.

"Samir, darling." She kissed my cheek. "How are you doing?" The voice of the charmer. She had never used it on me before. I figured she wanted something.
"I'm doing okay, Wicked. The weather is somewhat depressing."
"Where are you going?" she asked me.
"Home."
She put her arm in mine. It made me somewhat uncomfortable. I steadied myself. It was time I told the truth. It was time I put the sign above my head. I am a homosexual. "Would you mind if I walked with you a bit? I want to talk to you about something."
"Sure thing," I said. "I wouldn't mind the company."

It was cold. We walked huddled together.
"I have a favor to ask you."
"What is it?" I prepared myself for what was coming. I am gay, I am gay, I practiced in my mind.
"There is this real cute guy I am interested in."
"Oh." I practiced nonchalance. I had not gotten used to a girl hitting on me.
"He is a great guy. I think he likes me, but I think he is gay."
"Oh, really?" This was proving difficult.
"Well, you know how it is. He treats me the same way you do. So I figured maybe you can help. I thought maybe if you met him,

you would be able to tell for sure. You know, the gay thing. You can tell each other and so on."

I started blushing. I had to pretend I was not shocked by what she was saying. It would be more embarrassing if she found out I did not know she knew I was. I was unsure how to proceed.

"I'm not sure I would be much help," I stammered. "I am not very good at telling."

"Are you a virgin, dollface?"

"No, of course not," came my quick reply.

"Well, you're acting like one, darling!" She looked at me intensely. I realized I was in over my head.

"I am not a virgin," I said emphatically. I should have added "technically." By that time, I had been with one female prostitute and four men; two of those times actually occurred in a bed. I had never been kissed. The sex I had had consisted of mutual masturbation and receiving oral sex twice. I had convinced myself I would be able to relax sexually once I got over Karim. Unlikely, but I had convinced myself nonetheless. "I have been with a few men," I said.

"I think you will like Mark. He is really cute. I figure if I can't have him, you should. Maybe if you get laid, you'll stop looking so drab. You're the worst-dressed homosexual I have ever known. Did you know that?"

"I'll alert the media," I said sarcastically.

"You don't have to. Everybody knows already!"

I wondered if I could ever be as ebullient as she was.

She was right. Mark was gay. She invited both of us to a party at her flat, a crowded, raucous affair. I walked in, she took my arm and led me to Mark. I knew right away he was gay, the only one at the party. She introduced me by saying, "Mark, this is Samir. He's from Lebanon. I invited him just for you. I think you'd make a great couple. He's practically a virgin, so be gentle with him or I'll be on your ass." She left us there, both crimson red, stuttering, unable to believe what she just did. That was January 21st. Our anniversary.

————

My four brothers and I are having breakfast on a grand piano. I tell Farid, my eldest brother, that he needs ketchup on his meal. I pour the ketchup out of the bottle and onto his plate. I pour so much it overflows and drips down on the piano.

I sit on the piano to play. I try to play a chord. There are no black keys. The piano has only white keys. Nawal joins us. She sits next to me on the stool and asks me to play with her. The piano now has both white and black keys.

The six of us cut up the piano, divide it up among us, and eat it.

Siblings always divide up the pie.

————

Scott came home one day and told me the bookstore he was working at was up for sale. He was unsure what would happen to him, and his coworkers, if it were sold. His birthday was coming up, so I bought it for him.

————

An hour later. Arjuna and his charioteer, Krsna, on the battlefield. They are now joined by Jesus, Eleanor Roosevelt, Mame Dennis, Julio Cortázar, and Tom Cruise, who looks a little lost.

ARJUNA: Hear my cry, O God; attend unto my prayer. From the end of the earth will I cry unto thee, when my heart is overwhelmed: lead me to the rock that is higher than I. For thou has been a shelter for me, and a strong tower from the enemy. I will abide in thy tabernacle for ever: I will trust in the covert of thy wings.

KRSNA: That's nice.

ARJUNA: You don't hear me. In an ordered world, you would hear me.

JULIO: This world is a mess, unbridled chaos.

JESUS: I hear you. If you pray to me, I hear you. I am the alpha and the omega.

KRSNA: Just shut up. Stop trying to confuse the boy. This world is fucked up as it is without you trying to fuck it up some more.

ARJUNA: But he may have the answer. He may know what the meaning of life is.

JESUS: I do. If you worship me, I will give you all the answers. I am the alpha and the omega.

MAME: Is this guy for real?

JULIO: Of course not. He just shows up to distract people. He's loads of fun, though.

ARJUNA: I wish someone would just tell me what it's all about.

MAME: Live, you fool. Life is a banquet and most poor suckers are starving to death.

KRSNA: Go out and kill your cousins.

MAME: Live, live, live.

JULIO: Kill, kill, kill.

TOM: I'm horny.

ELEANOR: Oh, shut up.

———

Operation Grapes of Wrath.

Where do they come up with these names, I wonder? Desert Storm and Desert Shield. I still like Kurt calling it Operation Panty Shield.

Operation Grapes of Wrath killed about 150 Lebanese, which is relatively minor in the history of the Lebanese wars. The operation did help unify the Lebanese for a little while. Israel's bombing of the UN base outraged the Christians, even though the majority of those killed were Shiites. For the first time since a February 1994 bombing of a Catholic church north of Beirut killed ten people, there were displays of unanimity among the various citizens of my country.

Black-robed Maronite bishops stood by turbaned Shiite clerics during the funeral in Qana, site of the massacre. There was a mass grave for 103 people. The precise number of the dead was unknown since many of the victims had been so blown to pieces and disfigured by the shells and the ensuing fire that they were not complete corpses. There were no foreign dignitaries at the funeral. If it were 103 Israelis that were killed in a shelter, would the world have been so silent?

The Shiite clergyman told the world, "The Jews committed a holocaust in Lebanon."

The old Lebanese proverb still holds. My brother and I against my cousin, my cousin and I against the stranger. Just let me hate somebody.

The Grapes of Wrath.

———

Remember me. Remember me, please. Please remember me. Please.

Forgive me.

———

When Scott was hospitalized the first time with PCP, Mo and I became closer. The wall he kept hiding behind went down. He became an integral part of my life.

He was the first person to tell me my paintings were bad. The funny thing was I was not devastated by his harsh criticism. I always thought I was so insecure about my painting I would be devastated by criticism. I guess I was lucky in the beginning. For the first eighteen months or so, everybody liked my paintings. Some said they did not understand them, but even those who said so, said they liked them anyway. In the first eighteen months I was in four group shows, two of which were juried. That was quite a feat. I was very proud. I even had a solo show at an alternative gallery, the second floor of a nondenominational church. I invited everybody I knew to the reception. All showed up. Even the artists I knew made sure to emphasize what a great show it was. Mo did not show up till about fifteen minutes from when the reception was supposed to end. I had been waiting for him the entire time. I wanted to tell him I started painting because I had seen his exhibit and it inspired me.

Everybody knew who he was. I saw the gallery curator prepare to go meet him. He came in, barely glanced at the paintings, before turning around to leave, not saying anything to anyone. I caught up to him as he was going down the stairs. I asked him why he was leaving so fast. He said he hated openings. He made an appearance because I asked him to. I asked him what he thought of my work. I will never forget the way he looked at me, as if he was wondering whether I could handle it.

"Your paintings suck," he said. Just like that. I smiled nervously, trying to cover up my embarrassment. It was the wrong reaction. He left shaking his head.

I agreed with him. For the entire time I was painting, I was doing it because I loved the fact I could call myself an artist. People were always impressed by that. I was also doing it because I loved painting, but deep down I realized I knew nothing about art. I always felt like a fake when someone complimented my work. I became somewhat arrogant to compensate for my insecurities. In one blow, he forced my hand.

He did not mention my paintings for a while. About a week later, I went to visit Scott. Mo was in his studio painting. I walked in and he did not stop painting. I sat and watched. I was entranced. The painting was a representational 60 by 80, three men and a woman, sitting at a kitchen table. There was a woman standing on the side, frontal view, lifting her skirt up and peeing. She had male genitals. On the kitchen table were a book, a hypodermic needle, and a .357 magnum.

I saw the brush move all around the canvas, as if it had a mind of its own. He rarely looked at his palette. He mixed colors on the canvas itself. He carried a dirty rag in his left hand and would wipe out entire parts of the canvas in one swoop. There would be four people at the kitchen table, then there would be three. The skirt would come down, then it would go up. Nighttime, daytime. Day turned into night and I was still sitting there watching. He had been painting for over nine hours straight, and I had sat there and watched. I had a couple of bathroom breaks, but he had none.

He did not stop on his own. Scott came in and said dinner was ready. Mo said he did not want any dinner. Scott took the brushes Mo was using and threw them in the garbage can. Mo cursed as he dug through the garbage for his brushes. He put them aside and went to wash up for dinner.

The next day, I started a new painting. I tried a portrait of Juan, who had just died. I could not draw very well, so it never really looked like him. I finished it in about a week. I liked the result. It was not like anything I had done before. I gathered all my courage and took it to Mo's studio. He said it was awful. He took me to the San Francisco Museum of Modern Art and sat me down in front of a David Park. I was not to move from my seat for at least an hour. He left me there.

I started another painting, a portrait of Steve, who had also just died. I finished it in about three days. I thought it was a much better painting than Juan's. I took it over to Mo. He said it was terrible. He sat me down with a book of Rembrandts. I could not understand why he would want me to look at that book since I could not paint like that in a million years. He closed the book and took it away. I had to beg him to give it back.

He thought my third painting was a piece of shit. He said I was regressing. He explained to me some things about composition. My fourth painting was disgusting. My colors were all wrong. Back to the Museum of Modern Art for an hour in front of Matisse. My fifth painting was nothing short of repulsive. It must have been done by a blind man. Vermeer to study aesthetics.

I gave up. There was no way I could paint. Seeing all those great paintings had discouraged me. I could never do what those painters did. That was when my mother passed away. A month passed and I did not show Mo any paintings since I had not done any. He probably assumed it was because my mother had died. I could not tell him I was not going to paint anymore. He never mentioned my painting during that time.

My paints were still out. A blank canvas stared at me every night. I decided to do a last painting of my mother. I finished it in one night. I thought it was a weak painting, but I loved it. The composition was not very good. The drawing was actually bad. The color was muddy because I had used so much paint, except for a small red stroke which I thought was a stroke of genius. I sarcastically convinced myself that one stroke of genius could make a painting work.

I took my painting to Mo. He looked at it for a while. All he said was, "That's not bad." I broke into tears. I sobbed like a baby. He got upset, stood up, and screamed, "I didn't say it was any good.

I just said it's not bad. What's the matter with you?" He left the studio in a huff. I kept crying.

Scott put his head through the door, smiling from ear to ear. "He liked it, huh?"
"He said it wasn't bad," I choked between sobs.
"Ooooh, he liked it. He liked it."

———

"Are we merely blind brutes loosed in a system of mindless energy, impotent, misdirected, and insolent?"
"No," Coover says aloud, "we are not."
"We are," I say.
"We're not," he insists.
"We are."
"We're not."
"We are."
"Not."
"Are too."
"Not."
"Are too."
I stick my tongue out at him. He is so petulant.

———

"Did you check out his socks?" Georges asked his friends.
"No," replied the dark-haired fighter. "Were they good?"
"They were great, Ted Lapidus."
"If you want them, you would have to go down and get them," the other boy said.
"I think I will." Georges athletically jumped over the bridge, landing on the soft ground two meters below. He walked under the bridge where they had stacked up the bodies. Finding what he

was looking for, he took off the corpse's shoes, making sure the socks didn't get any mud on them. The socks in his pocket, he climbed back up to his position on the bridge.

"Did you find them?"

"I sure did," Georges said, taking the offered cigarette from his friend.

Another car was approaching the barricade. He stood up, released the safety from his machine gun. The car stopped, window opened, driver smiled nervously.

"Identity card," Georges ordered.

———

When he opened the seventh seal, there was silence in heaven for about half an hour, which was really a good thing because any kind of noise would make the soufflé drop, and there is nothing worse than a flaccid soufflé, is there, Jezebel darling? Fallen! Fallen is the great soufflé! Fallen! Fallen is Babylon the Great! From the sky huge hailstones of about a hundred pounds each fell upon men. And they cursed God on account of the plague of hail and the fallen soufflé.

I saw heaven standing open and there before me was a white horse, whose rider is called Faithful and True. He was at Bloomingdale's trying to return the seven lampshades, but the salesclerk would hear none of it. "I am the alpha and the omega," he kept repeating. "Well, Mr. Alpha," she said in her Puerto Rican accent, "the sign says no returns without a receipt. Can't you read?"

Balak sighed. In Laodicea, there were no soufflés to be found. "Woe! Woe, O great city, dressed in fine linen, purple and scarlet, and glittering with gold, precious stones, and pearls! In one hour such great wealth has been brought to ruin. So where is my fucking soufflé?"

July 5th, 1996
Dear Diary,

Today would have been Samir's thirty-sixth birthday. I was unable to stop crying all day. What a fucked-up world we live in. What a cruel, cruel world. What a cruel God or what an incurably frivolous God.

———

Everybody came to stay with us in the summer of 1982, everybody. Grandma Nabila and Grandpa Boutros, Uncle Yousef, his wife and three kids, Aunt Fawzieh, her husband and four children, Uncle Mustapha, his wife and three children, and Aunt Lina. That made twenty-one of us in the house. They stayed with us until the PLO left in late August.

It was very strange. I was an only boy. The house was just for my mother and me since my father died. Having all these kids staying in our house was strange, not bad, just strange. I had to share the sofa with my cousin Zuhair. I would sleep on one end and he on the other, and our legs met in the middle to do battle. He was thirteen, a year older than I was. He was the first one to play with my penis.

Uncle Mustapha was furious all the time. The Israelis were everywhere. Their big guns were all around us bombing West Beirut. He would look out the window to see the tanks, no more than a hundred meters away, shelling his home. The Israelis laid siege to West Beirut for a long time. We all watched. Grandpa Boutros was never as upset as his son. He just kept saying everybody was crazy, which was true, of course.

I got used to having everybody around. My cousins and I created all these different games to play during the day, and at night Zuhair and I came up with even more games. So on the day the PLO agreed to the Israeli demands, I was a little disappointed that everybody would leave. The Israelis did not stop bombing after the agreement, however. They kept firing a long time after that. Everybody waited till the day the PLO left Beirut before they went home because Uncle Mustapha kept saying the Israelis would keep shelling no matter what they agreed to. When they left, it turned out only Aunt Fawzieh's home was completely destroyed.

Zuhair and I never played penis games again. He found better things to do with it, I presume. I did not.

————

NAWAL: *(putting the coffee cup down)* So how's your love life these days?

KURT: Don't ask!

MARWA: She just did.

NAWAL: This is good coffee.

KURT: I don't mind talking about it. There is not much to talk about. I don't have one and it's not because of lack of trying. It's just difficult to find someone to have any kind of relation-ship with.

NAWAL: There are a lot of men in the city who are in a
            similar health situation. Isn't there some so-
            cial group or gathering where you can meet
            other guys?

KURT: There are lots of them. It's just not conducive
            to salacious trysts.

NAWAL: What do you mean?

KURT: When two men in my health situation get to-
            gether, it isn't very erotic. It just isn't, no mat-
            ter how much we may want it to be.

MARWA: Why is that?

KURT: Oh, I don't know. It just isn't. Just yesterday
            I met this guy. We were supposed to get to-
            gether for the sole purpose of having sex, and
            it didn't happen.

MARWA: What happened?

KURT: We had talked on the phone. He had left a
            message on a phone sex line saying he was
            looking for a nice guy to have sex with. He
            said he was HIV-positive. Well, I left him a
            message and he called me back. We got
            along great. We could not get together right
            away. He kept leaving me these messages
            and I began hesitating, thinking he was a
            little too desperate. That's funny, right? Me
            thinking someone else is desperate. Anyway,

146

he finally called me the day before yesterday. He left a long message on my machine telling me what he was going to do to my hard dick when we got together. Well, we got together yesterday. We decided to meet right here in this coffee shop. When he first showed up, I realized he was not my type, but I thought he was a nice guy anyway and I would go to bed with him. *(Pause. Drinks coffee.)* Anyway, he sat down and I asked how he was feeling. He said he was feeling kind of queasy. I asked him what he was taking. He started reciting the litany of drugs. He was on 3TC, D4T, and Saquinavir. He was also taking Acyclovir as a prophylactic against herpes. Septra for pneumocystis, Sporanox for fungus. The list was endless. About as long as mine actually. We started comparing drugs. Is Saquinavir better than Crixivan? Isn't it hell to have to eat three meals a day, making sure you drink a glass of grapefruit juice with each meal to be able to take Saquinavir. Let me tell you, if we had a single lascivious thought in our mind, it was gone after the first ten seconds. Hell, I started feeling queasy. Twenty minutes later, he just stood up and said, "It was nice meeting you. See you later." That was it.

NAWAL: God, that must be tough.

KURT: It is. It really is tough.

MARWA: It might get better.

KURT: *(smiles gently at Marwa)* No, dear, it only gets
                         worse.

MARWA: I'm sorry.

———

Beirut was the center of the Arab world. It also was the most
Western and modern city in the region, even more so than Tel
Aviv. American, French, and national schools taught three languages, Arabic, French, and English. Both Middle Eastern and
European history were emphasized. Arabs, Europeans, Americans, Asians, and Africans, lived and worked in the city. The
regional branches of all international banks, multinational corporations, and the regional headquarters of all the international
press were located in Beirut. Lebanese banks considered only
the Swiss as their competition.

Theaters alternated Arabic plays with Western ones. They showed
American, English, French, and Arabic films, as well as kung fu
movies, of course. Television shows were never dubbed. French
shows were subtitled in both English and Arabic, and English
shows were in French and Arabic. Even taxi drivers spoke a little English and French, with the native Arabic.

There was a free press, and political ideas and criticisms were
bandied about endlessly without inhibition. The schools and the
universities were the best in region, and so were the hospitals.
Doctors and university professors were educated at home or
abroad, and they were both nationals and foreigners.

The tourist trade flourished. The hotels were top-notch. Exquisite restaurants were open twenty-four hours. The Casino du Liban

was world-class. The mountains provided ski resorts in the winter and cool summer resorts during the hot months in Beirut for those who had their fill of swimming in the Mediterranean.

Mosques and churches stood literally side by side. Seventeen different religious groups, Muslim and Christian sects, a Druze and a sizable Jewish community, flourished in Beirut.

Then a war began.

———

Winter of 1980. I was still living in Paris. Nineteen years old and naïve as can be. I was walking in one of the many *passages* off rue Montmartre when I spotted a sign that said *Hammam pour Hommes*. A men's Turkish bath sounded exciting. I went in to investigate. It cost a lot to enter, which surprised me. The attendant gave me a locker key, attached to a cloth bracelet to tie around my wrist.

I entered through the double swinging doors, like saloon doors in an old Western movie. John Wayne swung the doors and burst through. In reality, it was more like Beaver Cleaver putting his head through the doors to make sure it was safe. The locker rooms had a number of men in various stages of undress. Exciting. I felt uncomfortable as they stared at me. I couldn't even look back, no furtive glances even, my usual fare when in locker rooms. These men were not behaving normally. They were openly staring.

I was undressing when a Lebanese man walked in. I could tell he was Lebanese right away. He opened the locker right next to mine. He was a typical Lebanese if there was such a thing. Perfumed, well dressed, and tons of jewelry. It took about ten minutes for him to remove the rings, the chains, the bracelets, all manly jewelry. He was wearing a wedding ring.

In my locker was a towel. When I took it out, my mouth dropped. It was long enough. I could wrap it around my waist twice, but it was so short it barely covered my butt. It was then I realized this was a gay place. I was so naïve. I looked up and for the first time I saw fat men, with towels barely covering anything, walking by, staring at me. I thought about getting dressed and leaving. I gathered my courage and stayed. I should at least look around.

The *hammam* had apparently a number of floors, all underneath the ground floor where I had entered. It was as if it was going into the bowels of the earth. I looked around the ground floor— two locker rooms, a bar, a sauna, and a shower room. There were two small rooms with small cots where the lighting was so bad one could hardly see. I did not figure out what they were for till later.

The floor below had toilets and a steam room with accompanying showers. I kept going down, and the next floor had another sauna, a swimming pool, and a Jacuzzi. It was on this floor I woke up and realized what this place was all about. Through a badly lit entryway, I got into another dark area. A sign said VIDEO ROOM, so I went in to see what was in there. It was a gay porno video, and men were sitting close, masturbating each other. I closed the door in a hurry. As I walked through the entryway, I saw the same dark rooms as on the floors above, but these were not empty. Some doors were closed and others had naked men, in various positions, who looked at me, pleading with me to join them. I pretended not to notice, but I was suffocating. What if someone saw me there? The last room was the pièce de résistance. It was larger than the others, darker even. I first saw shadows moving slightly, but as my eyes adjusted to the darkness, I saw a group of no less than ten men in some form of sexual position which I am still trying to un-tangle to this day. What caught my eye was one boy, probably my age or younger, riding at least one penis, his face in pure ecstasy, his mouth open, forming a vowel of some sort, looking as if he was about to commence singing the *"Marseillaise."* He happened to glance my way, and our eyes locked. His eyes asked me to join him. I broke away, running.

I hurried back up. I was nervous as hell and wanted to get out of there. As I hurried up the stairs, I saw the Lebanese man. He was sitting between two other Lebanese men on a sofa. They were ogling me as I was coming up. He said to the other two in Arabic, "Look at this one. He is so beautiful." I felt myself flush all over. I had to pretend not to understand what he said. I got an erection and my hands went down to cover it, since the towel was not much help. "I sure could fall in love with this one," the other Lebanese said. I quickly went by them, continuing up to the ground floor. "What an ass! What a beautiful ass! I could fuck that ass all night." By the time I reached my locker, I thought every-body could see how red my face was. Everybody must have seen how hard my erection was. I must have set a record with how fast I dressed and ran out of there. That was the only time I had ever been to a bathhouse.

I have tried to explain to Mark why I consider that experience going up the stairs the most erotic of my life. I have never been able to. I have never been able to understand it myself. I realize my sexual experiences are very limited, yet try as I might, I can't seem to figure why some lecherous countrymen in a bathhouse, admiring me and my physique, would turn me on so much. All I have to do is think of that experience and I get tingly and flush all over. I have never had sex with a Lebanese. I have never had sex in Lebanon. The only Lebanese I was ever attracted to was Karim and I am not sure that was really sexual.

I am at a loss to explain it.

———

Everybody knows how inefficient government agencies like the U.S. Postal Service or the DMV are, but when it comes to the Centers for Disease Control, they somehow think it is not a bureaucracy. The CDC is simply the post office with white lab coats.

———

They forget about us. Israel attacks Lebanon, it is front page news. They kill children in an ambulance, it still is news. They bomb a UN shelter killing 105 civilians, it gets reported. The fighting goes on for a week, it gets moved back to page three. It goes on for two weeks, more people die, and it is no longer news.

It's a short attention span.

When did the last AIDS story make a newspaper's front page? My friends die. They keep dying, but people forget. Life goes on.

People forget. They forget who Assad is. Americans forget Assad killed twenty thousand of his own people by having his air force bomb Hamma, their own city. They forget all the terrorist groups he helped foster. In the new world order, he is a major player.

The Christians forget they begged the Syrians to get involved in Lebanon. They were losing the war. When the Syrians invaded, the Druze fought them in the mountains. A while later, it was the Christians who fought them valiantly. The Druze became allies of the Syrians, even though they killed their spiritual and political leader. They too forget.

We all forget. We become pawns in a game we don't understand. Drug companies sell us drugs which won't heal us, but we need them. Money comes and goes, but we don't see anything resembling a cure. We forget Israel used nail bombs in Lebanon, bombs which sent nails flying all over the place. We forget Syria massacred one thousand Lebanese soldiers in Ba'abda. The war stops, and starts again, and we forget about it.

The Israelis forget. They forget Pierre Gemayel started the Phalange party, naming it after Franco's fascist party. They forget that Pierre's idols were Hitler and Mussolini. Pierre and the Israelis became best friends.

Assad cannot afford a peace settlement. He prods Peres into a war he can't win. They both sit on the sidelines, shrugging shoulders. People die, and it is no longer newsworthy.

Assad kidnaps and tortures thousands of Lebanese. Warren Christopher wants to negotiate with him. Peres kidnaps and tortures thousands of Lebanese. Christopher kisses his ass.

The Lebanese forget. Syrian rule is better than Christian rule, and Israeli rule is better than Muslim rule. Drug companies ring their cash registers. Reagan sleeps well at night. He has forgotten everything.

Welcome to my world, motherfuckers.

———

I am standing in a hospital room. There are three beds, each with emaciated men dying. The men are uncovered, wearing flimsy hospital gowns. Each has his own IV stand next to his bed. The room has two large windows through which a bed, with a fourth dying man, can be seen on the ledge outside.

A woman stands in the middle of the room. She has black hair and black eyes, but is very light-skinned, pale. She is very thin and looks good in a long black dress.

"I believe you forgot some money a while back," she says. I realize she is right. I could not remember the amount, but I had not taken all of my money out of a bank when it left town. I did not bother since it was a piddling amount. "It has grown because of interest through the years, of course," she says. "Let's look at how much you have now."

She moves to the window and opens it. She pulls in a large black suitcase. She opens it. "Oh my," she exclaims. "You now have $582,262.23." The suitcase is full of money. I am so happy. She is so happy for me. She hugs me. All enveloping. I feel so good.

———

In reality, Lebanon has no mail service. It never did. A postal service does exist, but I doubt anybody knows why. Like most government bureaucracies, it is completely incompetent. The only thing the Lebanese postal service has in common with its American counterpart is a penchant for sophisticated assault rifles in killing people. Of course, in Lebanon, this is by no means exclusive to postal workers.

Although some streets have names, most houses or buildings do not have numbers. An address with a number and street would be a complete mystery. When filling out various government forms, addresses would appear something like this:

MR. ALAA ABU NABI AND FAMILY,
6TH FLOOR, AMIN BASTAWI BUILDING,
NEXT TO THE BIG FISH MARKET,
(PHONE NUMBER 860 634)
AISHE BAKKAR, BEIRUT

Still, even with such a clear address, the mail is rarely delivered. To get any kind of mail, one needs a post office box, and a hefty bribe to the head honcho at the post office in which one's box is located.

———

My sister turned out to be unlike any of us, intelligent. In our family, that was a noncompute. She sat for her Baccalaureate exams when she was fifteen. At sixteen, she was studying philosophy at the American University of Beirut. My father had numerous fits of androcentric apoplexy. He felt it was an egregious affront against the family. He eschewed his usual laconic speech patterns for unending diatribes, which he really should have simply recapitulated into "What man would want to marry a woman smarter than him?"

My eldest brother, Farid, believed she needed an education, which my father probably thought was heretic. When the fighting grew heavy again, he paid for her trip to New York and arranged for a minimal monthly stipend. It was minimal because she had a full scholarship at Columbia.

I do not know if Farid would have helped her had he known she was to meet me and move in. I would hope he would have. He is twelve years older than I.

Nawal finally got her Ph.D. from Stanford. She intends to go back to Beirut, after I die, of course. I do not see why. She kept going home at least twice a year throughout her college years. She was the family bridge.

———

May 17th, 1995
Dear Diary,

I don't know what is happening to my country. It is as if it is being torn in two. Everybody seems to be fornicating all over the place. The Department of Health floods the market with AIDS awareness ads, but none of the men seem to pay any attention. Condoms are considered unmanly. Prostitutes are readily available. Russian, Romanian, and Czech girls are selling their wares in Jounieh. Local Shiite girls are selling theirs in Al Dahieh. What a strange world this has become. Poor Shiite girls can make money in two ways, either by becoming prostitutes or by diapering themselves. It seems Iran pays two hundred dollars a month to any girl who puts on a diaper. I know I am insulting Muslim women everywhere when I call the traditional head cover a diaper, but it is so appropriate. Everybody here calls it that anyway. A diapered woman is one who covers her whole body except for her hands and face. Thankfully, no one here wears the Iranian black *chadors* where only the eyes can be seen. Maybe Iran would pay a thousand dollars a month if women wore that.

Prostitution or diapers? What a choice. What a crazy world we live in.

———

I was terrified. I had been depressed for months. My friends were dying. My blood results had been declining.

Something had to be done.

I flew to the high desert of Arizona, my haven. I said, "Father, can you help me?"

Father asked me if I was sure I wanted help. I tried to convince him. Father suggested that I spend three days in silence and fasting. No talking. No music. No food. No reading. Me, myself.

Father suggested I spend the time meditating. I was to calm my mind, repeating a mantra, *Sensa Uma*. Three days.

I was not much into meditating. My mind filled me with constant activity.

Sensa Uma. Sensa Uma. Sensa Uma.

I never really liked Sanskrit. My Western mind rejected it.

I was hungry.

Sensa Uma. Sensa Uma. Sensa Uma.

I was delirious. It was silly.

Sensa Uma. Sensa Uma. Sensa Uma.

I laughed hysterically. I spent a whole day laughing. Sanskrit, my ass. I regained my sense of humor. Sense of humor. Sense of humor.

My health improved.

———

I wanted to write a poem on my deathbed.

ON THE DEATHBED

Go, rest your head on a pillow, leave me alone;
leave me ruined, exhausted from the journey of this
     night,
writhing in a wave of passion till the dawn.
Either stay and be forgiving,
or, if you like, be cruel and leave.
Flee from me, away from trouble;
take the path of safety, far from this danger.
We have crept into this corner of grief,
turning the water wheel with a flow of tears.
While a tyrant with a heart of flint slays,
and no one says, "Prepare to pay the blood money."
Faith in the king comes easily in lovely times,
but be faithful now and endure, pale lover.
No cure exists for this pain but to die,
So why should I say, "Cure this pain"?
In a dream last night I saw
an ancient one in the garden of love,
beckoning with his hand, saying, "Come here."
On this path, Love is the emerald,

the beautiful green that wards off dragonsnough, I am losing
     myself.
If you are a man of learning,
read something classic,
a history of the human struggle,
and don't settle for mediocre verse.

I was unable to. Jalaleddine Rumi wrote much better than I ever
could, in the thirteenth century no less.

———

Laura answered the door. She tried to smile welcome. Not an
easy task. Eyes puffed, skin pallid, shirt stained. Taking care
of her brother was draining the life out of her. Succubus in ac-
tion.

We hugged. She told me Kurt was doing even worse. The doctor
was just there and he said Kurt would not make it through the
night. All medications were stopped. No IV. He was not in much
pain because the morphine patches had begun to kick in.

I held her in my arms as we walked the long Victorian corridor to
Kurt's room. Three friends of his were in the room, Sara, Jack, and
James. Kurt had many friends.

Kurt was snoring. I sat next to his bed. I did not want to disturb
him. He looked dead already. He opened his eyes suddenly.

"You're finally here," he said weakly.
"Yes, I am," I told him.
Laura came and sat on the other side. "Mo is here to see you,
Kurt," she said. "He's been here every day."

The others stood and surrounded the bed. No one wanted to miss anything. Something deep and meaningful might occur.

"How are you feeling?" Sara asked.

"You're finally here," he said weakly.
"Yes, I am," I told him.
"I need you to do something for me." His voice was barely coming through.
"Sure."
He took a breath. He was having trouble breathing. The final diagnosis was both KS and PCP in his lungs, possibly even CMV. No one was quite sure anymore.
"I want you to take my paintings." He began coughing. I had to wait. Sometimes it took a while. "I know they are not worth much. You can take care of them while I go on my trip."
"Are you sure you want me to take all of them?"
"Yes. I can't take them on my trip."

Jack jumped in. "What kind of trip are you taking, Kurt?"
Kurt didn't reply. He looked at me. I nodded my head. He smiled.
"Would you like anything for your trip?" Jack asked.
"A Coke," Kurt wheezed.
Jack looked at Sara, puzzled. Laura smiled for the first time. She asked her brother, "Do you want a Coke right now?"
"Yes."

She went into the kitchen to open a can. She poured some into Kurt's cup. I gave her my seat. She put the straw in his mouth. He tried to drink out of it and failed. Laura was ready for that. She took a needleless syringe from the night table. She filled it from the cup. She brought it close to his lips and he opened them on cue. She filled his mouth with Coke. He was able to handle two syringes.

He asked for music. Laura put on Van Morrison. We all listened. "I'm surprised he's still alive," Kurt said.

"Who? Van Morrison?" Sara asked.

"No," Kurt said. "My dad."

Kurt surprised everybody. He did not die that night. We all stayed with him all night. He stopped breathing at times, but came back. We took turns staying with him. Only Laura stayed with him all the time.

Two nights later, I was there with Laura and Sara. Kurt had had a rough day and we did not expect him to make it. We sat waiting. Sara got on my nerves. I would have said something, but she was a good friend of Kurt's. She kept talking to him about crossing to the other side, turning into a being of light, getting rid of his earthly body.

He was awake when she asked him if he still wanted to take his trip. "No," he said, "you changed my mind."

His moments of lucidity were rare. Laura was able to understand him most of the time for most of his conversations related to his childhood. I became Lucas, his best friend in kindergarten. He had not seen or heard of Lucas since he was five. He called Sara Jessica, his neighbor when he was growing up. He would look at Laura and tell her their mother was really upset with her. He had just talked to her and she told him Laura was misbehaving.

He did not die. Seven days later, he was still breathing, talking. He had not eaten in twelve days. No medication. He had not moved from his bed in over a month. Yet he still breathed. He died ten days after drinking Coke.

There was one incident two days before he died that summed up so much of how I felt about Kurt. Sara and Jack were in the room. Kurt woke up. Everybody looked at him.

"I wish," he said.
Sara perked up. "You wish?" she asked Kurt.
"I wish," he repeated.
Sara moved closer. Some pearl of wisdom might be forthcoming.
"I wish I was an Oscar Mayer wiener," Kurt sang the jingle. He then laughed to himself. I laughed so much I started crying.

———

Subject: Army curfew imposed on Beirut and other towns

BEIRUT, Feb. 28, 1996—A time-indefinite nationwide curfew was ordered by the Lebanese army. Army commander Emile Lahoud issued a statement saying that "a curfew is imposed on the cities of Beirut and its suburbs, Sidon, Tyre, Jounieh, Tripoli, Ba'albak, Nabatiyeh, Baaklin and Zahle as of 3 A.M. Thursday morning until further notice. Troops will open fire on anybody seen carrying a weapon if he does not respond to warnings."

Thousands of soldiers, armored personnel carriers and tanks took up positions and set up checkpoints in the capital's major squares, open spaces and road intersections as well as in Tripoli, Ba'albak, Tyre and Sidon. Among the security measures, entrances to refugee camps on the outskirts of Sidon would at least be tightly controlled and might be closed Thursday to prevent Palestinians from joining the demonstrations.

The army statement came after the CGTL (General Labor Confederation) called for protests during a general strike on Thursday. The CGTL represents 400,000 workers and is backed by opposition parties. The CGTL is asking for a 76 percent pay rise for workers and a 100 percent increase in the 250,000 Lebanese pounds ($157) monthly minimum wage, it is also demanding the cancellation of a 1993 ban on street protests and of a decision to decrease the number of private TV and radio stations. The labor union has become increasingly critical of Hariri's government which is seen as ignoring the needs of the poorer classes in Lebanon, while at the same time raising multibillion dollars to fund reconstruction projects.

Hariri rejected all the CGTL's demands on Tuesday and put the army in charge of public security and to stop street protests. Hariri said, "We will not allow the government to be toppled from the street." Newspapers called the government's decision to have the 50,000-strong army maintaining public order for three months a "partial declaration of martial law." The decision also puts General Lahoud in control of internal security forces totaling another 50,000 men. Last July authorities used troops and police to block street protests over tax and price hikes.

The CGTL leader, Elias Abou Rizk, said it would observe the curfew—apparently defusing a showdown with the government.

———

"So have you ever been in love?" I asked.
"Not really. Infatuated, quite a few times, but I don't think I have ever been in love."
"Liar," Marwa said softly. I did not think she was paying attention. All three of us were in my studio. She was labeling my paintings.

My sister sat in front of me, looking at the new slides. The morning light filled the studio. I should not have taken a break from painting, but lately I have been getting tired.

"I loved him, but I was not in love with him," my sister went on, not lifting her eyes from the slides. "You were the one in love with him."

"Rewriting history, are we? Sure, I was in love with him, but so were you."

"Are you guys going to tell me?" I asked.

"There is nothing to tell, really," my sister replied.

" 'Why won't he kiss me?' " Marwa used a high whiny voice. " 'Why? Why? My heart hurts so much.' " She clutched her bosom, embellishing the drama. "Not in love with him, my ass. You would have slept with his mother if she could have gotten him to go out with you. Come to think of it, it wasn't his mother, you went after his grandmother! 'Oh, Auntie Nabila, your cooking is so marvelous.' "

She ducked to avoid the flying pillow. This was turning out to be more amusing than I could have hoped for.

"Are you going to tell me or what?" I asked impatiently.

"I was not in love with him. I was just infatuated. That's all. I was fifteen."

"He was so cute," Marwa added. "Those eyes were killers. And that blond ponytail, oh, my God!"

"We both liked him a lot," Nawal continued. "He lived in Ba'abda with his mother, but came to West Beirut all the time."

"His father was killed by the Syrians when he was young. The fuckers then completed it. In 1989, they shelled his house killing both him and his mother."

"I'm sorry to hear that," I said. I was.

"I cried for a month when I heard," my sister said. "I guess I was in love with him."

"I was so in love with him," Marwa continued. "I kept dreaming of him even after he died."

"He was gay, you know." My sister was now looking at me. The slides were done with, on the coffee table.

"Really?" I asked.

"Yes," Marwa answered. They finished each other's sentences. "He told your sister after she tried to rape him."

"Oh, really?"

"I did no such thing. I just wanted him to kiss me. He told me he was gay. That's why I say I was not in love with him. How can you be in love with someone if there is no chance in hell you can sleep with him?"

"Why don't you ask your brother about that one?" Marwa looked at me, raising one eyebrow, a wicked grin plastered on her face. It was my turn to throw the pillow across the room.

———

Subject: Seven raising antigovernment signs are released.

BEIRUT, Feb. 26, 1996—Seven people were arrested on Friday as they were carrying antigovernment street signs. On Monday, Judge Nada Dakroub dropped the charges for incomplete evidence and said the signs were seized in a different area from where the suspects were arrested.

Raising street signs in Lebanon requires the approval of the interior ministry.

Death comes in many shapes and sizes, but it always comes. No one escapes the little tag on the big toe.

The four horsemen approach.

The rider on the pale horse says, "Hey, Diego, do you think this one is worthy?"

Velázquez, on the black horse, says, "This good and faithful servant deserted his country."

"Whoa," I interrupt heatedly. "You guys are diverging from the script."

Mondrian, on the red horse, says, "No. You diverged from the script. You used green in your paintings."

Jesus, on the white horse, says, "I curse you, Peter Rugg. For all of eternity."

The crotchety white rider leads the other three painters away.

I still have no feeling in my fingers. I can't touch home.

———

Time is the substance from which I am made. Time is a river which carries me along, but I am the river; it is a tiger that devours me, but I am the tiger; it is a fire that consumes me, but I am the fire.

Jorge Luis Borges is dead, dead, dead. Yet, he continues to whisper sweet nothings in my ear, promises of eternal love.

———

I always thought AIDS should be a trademark of Burroughs Wellcome. You know, AIDS™ is a registered trademark of Burroughs Wellcome, use of this trademark without paying royalties to its rightful owner is a crime punishable by a slow, tortuous, torturous death.

How much money has this company made on our suffering? How much money have the doctors, pharmacists, and various medical personnel made? Did anybody count? What about psychotherapists, and alternative healing practitioners? Viatical companies? I do not even want to consider the books published, the stories in the media. War profiteers.

Has anybody ever tried to figure what the average daily profit was? They did in Beirut. A local newspaper, *Al Diyar*, ran a cost estimate. A 240 mm shell cost $9,500. The 160 mm shell costs $1,500, the 155 mm $700, the 122 mm $300, and so on down to a single Kalashnikov bullet, which costs about thirty cents. In one night alone, an estimated ten thousand shells had poured down on the city. The cost estimate was about fifteen million dollars for one night. That is for one night of a war which started in 1975. How many years is that?

The Lebanese Civil War™ is a registered trademark of Martin Marrietta.

———

An hour later. Arjuna and his charioteer, Krsna, on the battlefield. They are now joined by Eleanor Roosevelt, Krishnamurti, Mame Dennis, Jalaleddine Rumi, Julio Cortázar, and Tom Cruise, who looks a little lost.

ARJUNA: My head hurts.

RUMI: All your agonies arise from wanting something that cannot be had. When you stop wanting, there is no more agony.

KRSNA: That's very well said. You hear that, Arjuna. If you understand that, life flows.

KRISHNAMURTI: Live your destiny.

JULIO: Stop trying to make sense of this chaos.

ELEANOR: Delete the need to understand.

MAME: Just live, darling. Stop trying to make sense of the book of life. It is a series of nonlinear vignettes leading nowhere, a tale, told by an idiot, full of sound and fury, signifying nothing. It makes no sense, enjoy it.

TOM: Are there any cute boys here?

ELEANOR: Oh, shut up!

———

August 7th, 1996
Dear Diary,

I shouldn't listen to music anymore. It makes me so sad. I should
stick to Arabic music. It is safer. If I listen to French music, I start
thinking of Samir.

I had the radio on in my car today. They were playing old songs
recorded by today's singers. Someone was singing "Let's Call the
Whole Thing Off." It's a funny song, or at least was funny until the
war. You say to-ma-to and I say to-mah-to. Well, that was what
happened during the war, except if you mispronounced tomato,
they shot you. Lebanese pronounce tomato *banadoura,* whereas
Palestinians pronounced it *bandora,* so the drivers of cars stopped
at Phalangist checkpoints were shown a tomato. If they mispronounced, it was *au revoir et merci.* Let's call the whole thing off,
so to speak.

It got worse for me as this singer with a gorgeous voice came on
singing Porter's "So in Love." It's a newer version I had never
heard. I remembered how Ella sang it. I used to love it as a girl.
When I was eleven, I was singing it when my father came into the
room. He listened to what I was singing. He came over and
slapped my face. He told me never to sing about love again. I was
furious in the car. I got so upset because he was so stupid. I got
so upset because I missed him so. When the song was over on the
radio, the announcer said this singer recorded the song to raise
money for AIDS. I had to stop the car and cry.

————

I had this story idea for a book. I had always been fascinated by
the mythology of Jesus, even though I was born a Muslim. The

book would lay out the life of the main protagonist, from birth to death, as a modern parallel to Jesus.

The main character—let's give him a real Muslim name, Ali—is born in Lebanon, the only son to his mother and father. The birth is miraculous. The mother was told she could never have a child. Ali grows up in an environment with an absent father—he works a lot—and a doting mother. A fairly typical upbringing for a mother-complected homosexual.

Childhood is relatively boring. We leave the story until his thirtieth birthday. He is living in the States. He has been infected with the virus, but is asymptomatic still. He has to be doing something dramatic. I would have made him a painter, but that is too obvious.

Let's have him be a fairly accomplished violinist. Through his exquisite playing he is able to move people to tears. He has a following.

One of his followers, a close friend, suggests that he should go back to Beirut and make peace with his father. He does. The father then sacrifices his son. He has him kidnapped in Beirut.

The final scene would have Ali tied spread-eagled, naked, face down on a bed. The father walks in. There are two kidnappers in the room. He tells his son what a disappointment he has been. He tells him maybe, if he dies, people would forget about his homosexuality. He nods at one of the kidnappers, who takes out a long knife. The description has to be subtle in pointing out the phallic implications. He then proceeds to stab the son between the shoulder blades. The father watches.

The father takes his son's bloodied corpse, wailing that he has been killed. Ali's mother, his only true love, cradles the corpse. Ali's death has exactly the consequence his father wanted. Ali becomes the most loved musician, a messiah. His father is idolized as the progenitor of a genius.

The book is written in the first person. It would be interesting to write, as the main character, the description of the knife stabbing me. I die. I find that so powerful. As the protagonist, I would be able to say, "Father, why have you forsaken me?"

Scott did not like the idea. He thought it was obvious, axiomatic.

———

I woke up hearing Marwa talking on the phone. She was crying. My sister was trying to understand what was happening.

It seemed Marwa's mother had talked to mine. They were not close friends, having little in common. Marwa's mother spent most of her time comforting Samir's mother after her son's death. My mother wanted nothing to do with it. It seemed that Najwa thought my mother should come over here and visit. She told my mother she had lost all three of her boys. My mother had already lost two. She should not allow the third to leave without saying good-bye. My mother said she considered that she had already lost three sons. It was easier that way. She always wore black.

Marwa told Nawal my mother was a bitch.

From my bed, all I could scream was "No."

The young driver opens the door of the white Range Rover. They whiz through all the checkpoints. The drive to Kaslik takes only about twenty minutes. The driver goes through a gate and parks in front of a hilltop house, overlooking the Mediterranean. The house is secluded.

The door opens as soon as the car arrives. He is waiting for her. He greets her with the perfunctory cheek-to-cheek kiss. He tells the driver to leave, he does not need him this evening. She thinks of complaining, explaining that she needs to go back later on. She decides against it. Why pretend? They both know her husband is out of town.

He leads her into the house. She is impressed. The view is breathtaking. She mentions it. He suggests they go out onto the verandah to watch the sunset. He pours both of them a Scotch. The Lebanese national drink. They both laugh. He brings the bottle with them as they sit to watch the sunset.

"I am glad you came," he says.
He is beautiful. She knows many men who are probably much more handsome, none as beautiful, though. She has never felt this way about a man.
"I'm scared," she says.
"I can see that." He smiles.
"I'm sorry." She laughs nervously. "I can't believe I'm here."
She tries to keep her eye on the view. He keeps his eyes on her. He refills her glass.

"You're trying to get me drunk, aren't you?"
"Yes, ma'am. Only a little."

"Can I kiss you?" he asks. She nods. A brief kiss. It tingles. She looks at him again. He does it again. This time, he touches her face. Tears roll down her face.

"He doesn't kiss you, does he?"
"Do we have to talk about him?"
"Just one question. When was the last time he made love to you?"
"Eight years ago."

She stands up and undresses herself in the open air. He looks at her, surprised. She wants approval. He smiles. He pulls her onto his chair. He begins the process.

———

In the name of God, the most compassionate, the most merciful:

23. But she in whose house he was, sought to seduce him from his (true) self: she fastened the doors, and said: "Now come, thou (dear one)!" He said: "(Allah) forbid! truly (thy husband) is my lord! he made my sojourn agreeable! truly to no good come those who do wrong!"

24. And (with passion) did she desire him, and he would have desired her, but that he saw the evidence of his Lord: thus (did We order) that We might turn away from him (all) evil and shameful deeds: for he was one of Our servants, sincere and purified.

25. So they both raced each other to the door, and she tore his shirt from the back: they both found her lord near the door. She said: "What is the (fitting) punishment for one who formed an evil design against thy wife, but prison or a grievous chastisement?"

26. He said: "It was she that sought to seduce me—from my (true) self." And one of her household saw (this) and bore witness, (thus): "If it be that his shirt is rent from the front, then is her tale true, and he is a liar!"

27. "But if it be that his shirt is torn from the back, then is she the liar, and he is telling the truth!"

———

"I made two thousand dollars last week."
"I don't want to hear about it," I say.
"No, Kurt, seriously. I am making a lot of money. Yesterday this man paid me a hundred dollars just to suck on my nipple for twenty minutes until he jerked himself off."
"I don't want to hear about it, Ben. I really don't."

He takes off his shirt and shows me his chest. "See anything different?" he asks.
"Huh?" is all I can come up with.
"See anything different?" he insists.
"How the fuck would I know?"
"I got rid of the KS scars."
"What are you talking about?"
"I tried freezing the scars. That worked, but it took a lot of time to heal. I now tattoo them."
"Tattoo?"
"Yeah. I tattoo the scars so nobody can tell. You know, tattoo them with my own skin color."

———

Marital intercourse is certainly holy, lawful and praiseworthy in itself and profitable to society, yet in certain circumstances it can prove dangerous, as when through excess the soul is made sick with venial sin, or through the violation and perversion of its primary end, killed by mortal sin; such perversion, detestable in proportion to its departure from the true order, being always mortal sin, for it is never lawful to exclude the primary end of marriage, which is the procreation of children.

Saint Francis de Salle, not the real Saint Francis with the cute birds and animals, wrote that in his book *Introduction to the Devout Life,* which talked about how bad sex was in four large volumes. It earned Francis here a sainthood. All I can say is, I am glad I'm not Christian. For us Muslims, we just stone adulterers to death, which is much more humane than guilt.

My brother Ibrahim was three years older than I. He was my closest brother in age. By the time I had left Lebanon in 1975, he was a member of the Murabitoun party, a leftist organization. I never realized he had become a member of their militia till he was killed a year later, one of the few attackers of Damour to actually fall. My father never forgave himself for letting my brother get so involved in the war. I was sixteen, in Los Angeles, away from it all.

When he kissed her, she kissed back. She tried to take his shirt off, but he had begun to move down. When he kissed her down there, a first, her body went rigid. When his tongue penetrated her, she lost control. Her hands instinctively went to hold his head in place. Her body rearranged itself to open up to his assault.

She had been naïve.

He spent an eternity down there. She kept calling for her mother. His tongue kept moving. She felt herself climaxing. She shook. She wept. He kept going. He looked up at her. "One more?" He smiled. She nodded, pleading. His tongue went back to work. She called for Mohammad.

She had been so naïve.

He moved back up. She tasted herself in his kiss. She tore his shirt off. He pulled his pants down. She held it in her hands. Too big. He penetrated her slowly. She wept. He didn't stop kissing her. Every time he moved out, she tried pushing him back in. Her nails dug into his back. She tried to swallow his tongue. He pulled back and looked straight into her eyes. He smiled. She could not stop smiling. She was his.

———

Sex is the last refuge of the miserable.

Quentin Crisp said that to Joan Collins, when he walked in on her having sex with Linda Evans. To cover up his embarrassment, he blurted out that statement, which made him famous all over again. And he should know.

———

I was horny. I walked into Badlands. I walked out with a boy. I took him home and fucked him silly. Great ass. He could not get enough. I fucked him three times. He wanted more. I wanted to sleep. I woke up to find him skewered on my dick. Sleepy as I was, my hips got into their ancestral rhythms.

"You're HIV-positive," he said.

"Yes, I told you that long before we got here. You said it was okay."

"No," he said, "I never heard it. I didn't know. I wouldn't have done what we did."

"What are you talking about?" I asked. "I told you yesterday and you said you didn't care, as long as it was safe."

"I don't remember that."

"Fuck this shit. Don't worry about it, babe, we were completely safe. Now get the fuck out of here."

I went to a tattoo parlor. I had them tattoo a large HIV+ on my chest, above my left nipple. No one can now claim I never told them.

I was asked by *ArtNews* to pose for a closeup photo of my chest with the tattoo. They thought it was an artistic statement. I did. The picture made the cover.

———

In the name of God, the most compassionate, the most merciful:

52. Now such were their houses—in utter ruin—because they practiced wrong-doing. Verily in this is a Sign for people of knowledge.

53. And We saved those who believed and practiced righteousness.

54. (We also sent) Lut (as an apostle): behold, He said to his people, "Do ye do what is shameful though ye see (its iniquity)?"

55. Would ye really approach men in your lusts rather than women? Nay, ye are a people (grossly) ignorant!

56. But his people gave no other answer but this: they said, "Drive out the followers of Lut from your city: these are indeed men who want to be clean and pure!"

57. But We saved him and his family, except his wife; her We destined to be of those who lagged behind.

161. Behold, their brother Lut said to them: "Will ye not fear ((Allah))?

162. "I am to you an apostle worthy of all trust.

163. "So fear Allah and obey me.

164. "No reward do I ask of you for it: my reward is only from the lord of the Worlds.

165. "Of all the creatures in the world, will ye approach males,

166. "And leave those whom Allah has created for you to be your mates? Nay, ye are a people transgressing (all limits)!"

———

There is nothing safe about sex. There never will be.

Norman Mailer told me that. He really was talking about his arch-nemesis, Truman. There is nothing safe about reading one of Norman's books. They induce narcolepsy. Do not drive, or operate heavy machinery while reading a Mailer book. Unless it is a good Mailer book, then all bets are off.

———

"Why do you have a gun under your pillow?" she asks.
"I have guns all around. Just in case."

He was lying in his bed holding her, her head on his chest, his left hand playing with her ass.

"Ouch," she moans.
"Does that still hurt? I'm sorry."
"Oh, don't stop. I like it."
"I thought you would." He laughed. He kissed her again. "When I first saw your picture, I knew you'd be a good fuck."
"When?"
"About a year ago. You were in the magazine *Ash Shabake*. It was a picture of you next to the asshole. You looked like you could use a good fuck."
"Do you always have to use that word?"
"Yes." He smiled.
"Have you killed people?"
"Are you sure you want to talk about it?"
"Yes."

"Oooh, haven't you had enough?" she asks.
"I love watching your face when I play with your pussy."
"Do you have to be this vulgar?"
"Yes." He smiled.

"You haven't answered the question."
"Yes, I have killed."

"Was it from afar or have you actually killed someone directly?"
"Both."
"A lot of people?"
"A lot of people."

"Are you sure you want to talk about this?" he asks.
"Yes. But please stop. I can't think when you're doing that."
"You're thinking fine." He smiles.

"Why?"
"It is wartime."
"That's not a reason. There are lots of men who are not killing."
"Not many. I am more honest."
"I don't understand."
"You will in time."

"Aren't you afraid of being killed?" she asks.
"All the time."

"Do you have a gun?" he asks.
"No, of course not."

He rolls on top of her, takes his hand out, and opens the drawer
of the nightstand. He takes out five pistols, one by one, places
them on her stomach, and rolls back over. His hand goes back to
its favorite position.

"I don't want a gun."
"You have to."
"Are they loaded?"
"Yes."
"You're crazy."

She pushes the guns away from her. He sits up, kneels, her legs around his waist. He picks up a gun and shows it to her.

"I think this would suit you."
"Okay."

He uses the barrel of the gun to massage her vaginal lips.

"It's loaded," she says.
"I know." He smiles.

The barrel penetrates. He moves it in very gently. The metal is cold. He explores with the gun. She can't say a word. She moans. He smiles. He looks into her eyes. She is his.

"Fuck me," she says.

He takes the gun out. He violently enters her. She thrusts up to meet him. The primitive cadence begins again.

She takes the gun from his hand. She points it at his face, her finger clutching the trigger. He smiles. He forces himself deeper. She moves the gun closer to his face. He licks the barrel. He tastes her. He puts the whole barrel in his mouth. He performs fellatio on the gun. She smiles. She looks into his eyes. He is hers.

She orgasms.

———

Kaposi's sarcoma.

The cancer was discovered originally among Mediterranean and Jewish men in 1871. Before AIDS, it was documented only in about six hundred cases in the last century. It usually struck Jewish and Italian men in their sixties. Purple lesions. With the onset of AIDS, the cancer was still discriminatory. It attacked only gay men, not hemophiliacs or heterosexuals, the most vain group of them all.

I am Mediterranean. I never got Kaposi's sarcoma. All my friends did.

I did contract toxoplasmosis and I fucking hate cats.

———

Scott arrived in San Francisco in early June, 1980. On June 29th, he attended his first Gay Freedom Day Parade. He loved it.

While standing and cheering the various contingents, he was approached by a thirty-two-year-old doctor. He fell in love. The doctor asked him if he wanted to party. Scott agreed.

The doctor gave him a pill.

The doctor took him dancing at the Galleria design center. Scott felt no pain. Five thousand people made it a tight dance floor. The doctor took off his shirt and threw it into the crowd. Scott danced. The doctor danced crotch to crotch. He undid Scott's belt. Scott felt the finger penetrate. He felt another hand playing with his ass. He felt a third.

They were at the Bulldog Baths. The doctor showed the *ingénu* the Bacchanalian delights.

Scott wanted to be kissed. The doctor tied him up, head down, with his ass up in the air. The doctor fucked him. And fucked him. But that was not the doctor. A third man had taken his place. A black man. A Latino. There was a line. The pleasure was constant. The most intense experience. In. Out. In. Out. Change.

At some point, during the night, the virus made his acquaintance.

The doctor did not call the next day.

I met Scott ten days later.

———

Lebanon is a piece of land (not a piece of heaven at all—you only have to be in Beirut in the summer) but it's *our* land, *our home* (even if actually we are not living there). It's our Sweet Home, and we *love* it. So we are called Lebanese.

———

August 12th, 1982
Dear Diary,

This is without doubt the worst day of my life. I can't take it anymore. The Israelis have gone stark raving mad. The planes started bombing at 6:00 A.M. and did not stop till 6:00 P.M. My nerves are shot. I don't understand what they want. They got everything. The Palestinians said they would leave. The Syrians are gone. But they still bomb us. What is it they want? Do they want us all dead? The PLO agreed to their terms. What more do they want? Haven't we suffered enough?

If her mother sees her now, she will have a heart attack and die. The driver keeps looking back at her in the mirror, smiling. She considers moving sideways so she does not have to see his eyes. Nick is between her legs, doing what he does best. She looks at the cars, as the white Range Rover speeds by. It is crowded on the highway.

———

It is pointless to describe in detail the exhibit at the Audrey Heller Gallery, Mohammad: The Last Paintings. Mere words cannot do it justice. It is exiguous, yet exquisite. It is minimal, yet unequivocally not Minimal, for it needs no manifesto or interminable elaboration. His style has become as laconic in statement as a parallel, as suggestively infinite. Mohammad is an imagist of cultural fugues and choreographies, of the faltering, lamentable Dance of Life. One pirouette is not the same as another, but there is no need to dance until one drops in a marathon. In painting, it is only necessary to outline the steps. Let the people dance!

———

I wonder if being sane means disregarding the chaos that is life, pretending only an infinitesimal segment of it is reality.

———

Mohammad: The Last Paintings, a posthumous exhibit, is a tribute to the painter's genius. It details a bittersweet account of a tumultuous life. It will assure him immortality.

I am in Berlin with my parents. We are on the street. We find out a parade is about to pass. I realize my parents might be embarrassed because it is a gay parade. It will raise issues they would rather not discuss. I am shocked, for I realize I am wearing women's clothing. I have a short wig on. No makeup, nothing flamboyant, just simple feminine stuff. It is pointless to change now for my father has already seen me as a woman. I take my wig off, for it becomes unnecessary.

———

My father is a good man, stuck in a cultural time warp. I find it hard to forgive him at times, until I am reminded how much I have grown up to resemble him. He wished his life to be simple, and due to circumstances beyond his control, it didn't turn out that way. He was a tyrant, softened up quite a bit with age, I hear, but he was always predictable. He laid down the law for everybody, and never deviated from it. I knew what the rules were. I knew that to be who I was meant a complete disinheritance, a complete disowning. I chose to be who I am today. It was never his fault.

———

I yearn for a moment I know nothing of.

I pine for a feeling, an impression of myself as content, fulfilled. At times, I feel it as a yearning for a lover, someone to share my life with, someone to laugh with. I loved, lost, and loved again. The longing never abated. I was only distracted for a little while. I searched for the elusive grail.

In that moment, I envision myself joyous, spiritually felicitous. When I shut my eyes, I feel the possibility of the moment. I long to understand.

Someday, I used to tell myself. Someday, I will know the moment I yearn for, someday.

I wait for the peace beyond all understanding.

I lie on my deathbed waiting.

I yearn for a moment I know nothing of.

––––––

"A work is never completed except by some accident such as weariness, satisfaction, the need to deliver, or death: for, in relation to who or what is making it, it can only be one stage in a series of inner transformations."
Paul Valéry was looking intently at me. Tired, I leaned back on the sofa. I needed rest.
"Do you think this is done?" I asked wearily.
"Sure," Paul replied. "You're dead. Your work is complete."
"Oh, good."

––––––

The Israeli planes flew so low the sonic boom shattered the windows. Marwa screamed.

"I don't want to stay here, Mom. Most of my friends have left."

"Okay," Najwa said. "I've decided. We're leaving. Go on and start packing."

"Good."

Najwa knew this was serious. The Israelis have been bombing Beirut, going unchallenged, for years. This time, everybody thought it would be more serious. The Israeli ambassador in London was shot the day before. No one claimed responsibility. The Israelis would be out for blood. For years, the bombing of "Palestinian targets" and "terrorist bases" had been nothing short of a calculated campaign to terrorize the Lebanese. It worked. She was terrified.

"If they did all that for one ambassador, what would they have done for two, Mom?"

They took a taxi to Damascus that afternoon. She could see, from the high vantage point of the mountains, the planes attacking. This was not going to be a simple cleaning up.

They were at her brother's in Paris when the reports started coming through. She should have known. Two weeks after the withdrawal of the Israeli forces from the Sinai, they invaded Lebanon. Whenever clouds gather in the Middle East, it rains in Beirut. The price of peace between Egypt and Israel was operation Peace for Galilee.

At least this time, Najwa will not have to go through it.

By the time the Israeli siege of Beirut was in full force, after thousands of Lebanese had died, a small report, in the back pages of the *Times* of London, stated that the Israeli ambassador had recovered fully.

March 14th, 1986
Dear Diary,

Today, I couldn't stop laughing. Three months ago the Swiss ambassador moved into the sixth-floor apartment of the building in front of ours. Every day at six, the maid would bring him a beer, which he drinks on the balcony. I have watched him do this every day. Today, for the first time, when he finished drinking his beer, he threw the bottle out into the empty lot below. I couldn't stop laughing. He is Swiss. Today, he became Lebanese.

———

Mohammad was talented. There was no doubt about it. As I began to study his paintings, I realized he was even better than I thought. Most of the art critics who reviewed his work were not Lebanese. I felt they missed quite a bit in his paintings. I learned a thousand and one new things about his painting from their writing, yet they never asked what we saw.

The Baltimore Museum of Art bought one of his paintings and had it on display. Mark and I drove over to look at it. The painting consisted of a simple image, an upside-down jackass, or donkey, floating in water, submerged, with only the legs showing. The perspective was looking down from a high angle at the jackass, in seemingly infinite waters.

It was a beautiful painting. The size was 60 by 80 inches.

The reviewers waxed lyrical. They eulogized the mythological symbolism of the image. The jackass was a symbol of devotion or a symbol of beginnings. It represented The Fool or Magic. The fact that it was upside-down could mean homosexuality. *Upside-down* and *invert* were once derogatory terms for homosexuals, one critic said. They wrote about the meaning of an animal exposing its belly. Surrender. The painting was about surrendering to the flow, surrendering to the unconscious, to life. The floating jack-ass was Zen-like. Since it was half-submerged, one critic suggested the artist was commenting on his mastery of both intellect and intuition, both technique and genius.

I do not have the acuity, or acumen, to pass judgment on what was written. I am not omniscient. I cannot comment on Mohammad's thought processes. He never talks about his paintings. I do know, however, something about the jackass. All Lebanese do.

The jackass should be considered Lebanon's symbol, its eagle. When I was growing up, you would see them all over the place, not as much in the large cities, but definitely in the villages and countryside. They were used for everything, from transporting villagers to plowing the olive groves. Everybody considered them stupid—jackasses, so to speak—yet they were methodical. I am positive most Lebanese would be outraged at the suggestion that the jackass be the national symbol, yet most of my memories of the mountains always include an image of a jackass, carrying a load or a villager, navigating the tortuous paths. The jackass as symbol of our peregrination.

I can already hear a Lebanese objecting to the jackass as symbol, since a Range Rover could do a better job.

As the civil war progressed, one would see less and less of the jackass. Whether they were easy targets for bullets or simply the victim of modernization, they no longer littered the mountain-side. It is a shame.

Maybe the art critics were right. The painting could have been about surrendering to life. It is possible everyone was right. The painting could comment about homosexuality, suggest that we surrender to life, and, at the same time, mourn the death of a country. I cannot say, for I know very little about art.

———

While in Paris, Marwa sent a letter to a teenage magazine asking for a pen pal in the United States. She was eleven. She received a sweet letter from a Sarah Miller, age thirteen, from Des Moines, Iowa. In the letter, Sarah told Marwa about her life. The chores she had to do, the cute boys she liked, the new mall that opened, and other exciting occurrences in the happening town of Des Moines. Marwa found it amusing.

Marwa and her mother were back in Beirut when school started again in the fall. She did not reply to Sarah's letter until she showed it one day to my sister, her best friend. The girls had cowritten a French essay a couple of months earlier, about the tragedy of growing up in war-torn Beirut. They had used overblown metaphors, preposterous tales of woe, and exaggerated sufferings. The essay was published in the Lebanese newspaper *L'Orient—Le Jour,* and was then actually picked up by *Le Figaro.* The girls translated the essay into English and sent it to Sarah. The return address was Marwa's post office box.

The next letter from Sarah brought fits of hysterical laughter from the girls. In the letter, Sarah exclaimed shock at what Marwa had had to go through. It included a thin piece of fruit cake, to ease the pain, Sarah said. The girls did not reply. That was followed a couple of months later by a letter which included a get-well card—Sarah said she could not find a more appropriate card since there was none that said anything about dealing with a war—signed by all her classmates. Sarah had read Marwa's letter to her class and they all wanted to help.

The girls never replied to Sarah. They had written only that one letter. Sarah kept sending letters, at least one every six months. In those letters she would empathize with the suffering of her "friend" and elaborate on what was happening in her life. Every letter included a little present to help Marwa through her suffering—a No. 2 pencil, a Mickey Mouse eraser, a hair net, a cookie, and so on.

The girls grew up. Both passed the Baccalaureate at the top of their class. They read how Sarah lost her virginity to John. They both studied overseas, Nawal at Columbia and Stanford, Marwa at Penn and Georgetown. They continued receiving letters from Sarah at the post office box.

I heard about Sarah only recently. My sister had just returned from Beirut. She was talking to Marwa on the phone, when I heard snippets about Sarah. I asked my sister about her. She gave me a brief synopsis, then showed me the latest letter Marwa was supposed to have received.

I opened the envelope and read the letter. Sarah was now considering marrying her college sweetheart. She was still in Des Moines. She was asking Marwa whether she should marry now or wait to make sure John was the right man. She asked about Marwa's well-being, hoping the constant war trauma was not affecting her adversely. She was including a little present to help ease her great suffering. I shook the envelope to see what kind of present. A single packet of blue lemonade Kool-Aid fell out.

She attended the funeral of Mr. Suleiman, at the Greek Catholic Church of Peter and Paul in West Beirut. Another funeral, another wasted life. Her husband sat next to her. She stood, she sat, obedient to the rites. It was a large funeral. She felt eyes on her. She discreetly turned around. He was watching her.

"Hello?"
"Hello beautiful."
"How could you show up? Why did you?"
"For a chance to see you in church."
"What if someone recognized you? Is it worth the risk?"
"Yes."
"You're crazy. If you wanted to see me in a church, all you had to do was say so. I would go to a church in Ashrafieh or Jounieh."
"Good. This Sunday then. We'll go together."
"Okay, but don't have any ideas about converting me."

"I'm going to kill him."
"No, you're not."
"Yes."
"No. You can't. I don't want to orphan my boys."
"I can take care of them."
"No. He's their father."
"They never see him."
"That's not true."
"I have been ordered, Samia. It's as good as done."
"No. No. You can't do it. Can't you tell them no?"
"It's from the top. He's gunrunning again."
"Oh, fuck."
"It'll be good for you."
"Is there any chance you can get them to change their minds?"

"No."

"I could tell him, you know. I could tell him that a friend told me your people are planning to kill him."

"It wouldn't make a difference. I would just have to go through more people to get to him."

"No. You can't do it yourself. You have to get somebody else."

"I want to do it myself. I have a hundred guys who could do it, but this one is mine."

"He has a bodyguard."

"I know."

"Don't hurt him, please. He is good-hearted."

"Okay. I promise I won't hurt him."

"Good. I like him. Don't let him see you. I would like to have him work for me."

"What about the driver?"

"Kill him."

———

Maria became our cook and housekeeper about a month after Scott moved in. She loved Scott and hated me. An obdurate Guatemalan, one of the few humans who refused to bow down to my temper. She was insolent and malapert with me, and the model of love and kindness with Scott. As he was dying, she sent her kids to her sister and moved in to be with him. When he died, I thought she would leave me. She did not. She remained as rude as ever.

One day, a year after he had died, I sat in the dark, crying. I heard Maria come into the room. She kissed the top of my head.

"It's okay," she said. "You have to forgive yourself. You did the right thing. It was what he wanted."

She left me there. She never mentioned it again.

———

In the cosmic circularity of the doctrine of the eternal return, Nietzsche forces together time and eternity. What is, has been, and will be innumerable times at immense intervals. Who gives a shit, I ask you?

———

I am in Beirut, sitting on my bed with Furball, Scott's Himalayan kitten. He is licking himself clean. My dad comes into the house with a female Great Dane. The dog comes over to look at the kitten, who is completely unperturbed. The dog bites the cat's head. I jump off the bed to get the dog to let go. I am not as fast as my father, who is already there, trying to open the dog's mouth. All I can see is the rest of the kitten's body, sticking out of the dog's mouth, a ball of fur. My father and I work together to free Furball. The dog, my father, and I move around in a circle. I notice my father is limping. He is the one wounded, not I. We finally are able to release Furball. He jumps back on the bed, and starts cleaning himself again, unharmed, unruffled. Every now and then, he looks at my father's bitch disapprovingly.

———

The explosion was heard in all of Beirut. The bomb was in Aishe Bakkar. Scores of people died, but that was not the intent. The Mufti, the religious head of our Sunni community, was killed in the explosion. His car was passing through the neighborhood.

That bomb killed my brother Hamid, his wife, and his three children, whom I had never met, on May 16, 1989. The building he lived in collapsed completely. I did not hear about his death till a year later. He was thirty-nine.

———

It took a while for me to realize I was in love with Mo. He is successful, intelligent, and unavailable emotionally. I always fell for that. It didn't help that he is tall, dark, and handsome, in a scruffy sort of way. He knew I was attracted to him and made no big deal about it.

I was Scott's ex, and there were quite a few of us, but of the group, only James and I became his friends. He made few friends, if any. In reality, most of the people in his life got there through Scott. He was at times completely unapproachable.

I never knew what went on between him and his father, but the one time I heard him talk about his father, I thought he was talking about himself. He said his father's friendships started by avoiding intimacies and eventually eliminated speech altogether.

———

All charismatic energy is basically sexual. John Kennedy, Adolf Hitler, or Jesus, it always was sexual.

———

"Hello?"
"Hey Mo."
"Hello, Kurt. How are you doing?"

"Not too well, but I think I'm feeling better today."

"I'll be over in the afternoon."

"Ha! That's what I am calling about. You had better not get out of the house today."

"Why?"

"Mo, Mo, Mo. You have to listen to the radio or turn on the TV sometimes. Your picture is all over the news."

"My picture?"

"Slight exaggeration. A composite drawing."

"Oh. Did we blow up something again?"

"The federal building in Oklahoma City. Scores of people killed. They are saying two of your people did it. It's a good thing you shaved your beard, huh?"

"Okay. Let me turn on the TV. I'll see you later."

"Bye, hon."

It looked like Beirut. They still think we're different.

It turned out an American did it. A true-blue American. No one explained how the wires came up with descriptions of the suspects as two Middle Eastern–looking men. No apologies, no explanations.

———

Easter. My favorite holiday. A deeply philosophical time of the year when I ponder what on earth a bunny rabbit has to do with eggs and why, if they beat you, spit on you, and nail you to a cross, you'd want to call that particular Friday a Good Friday? If that happened to me, I'd call it The Worst Friday of My Life. But that's why Jesus is The Redeemer and I'm just another nobody.

Resurrection is so seductive.

He was tied to the bedposts, spread-eagled. She squeezed his testicles, hard. His eyes twinkled.

"Tell me again."
"He begged me to spare him."

She squeezed again, harder.

"Tell me how. What did he say? You beg. Like he did. Maybe I'll spare your life."

He begged.

She kissed him.

―――――

Normality highly values its normal man. It educates children to lose themselves and to become absurd, and thus to be normal. Normal men have killed perhaps 100,000,000 of their fellow normal men in the last fifty years.

R. D. Laing, a British psychiatrist. Need I say more?

―――――

Backstreet was a bar on Makhoul Street. A tiny little place which was always packed, even on nights when shells were raining down. In any other part of the world, the place would have been closed for being a fire hazard. One entrance, the front, and three tiny windowless rooms on three levels, chock-full of people, a disaster waiting to happen. But who thinks of disasters in Beirut? There was nowhere to stand and it was difficult to move. Everybody was smoking. Jamal told him it was lucky they got in. He had to bribe the doorman. Samir cursed his luck.

Backstreet was owned by a man by the name of Philippe Duke. His claim to fame, and he was famous, everybody knew him it seemed, was he was Georgina Rizk's boyfriend when she became Miss Universe. When she was crowned Miss Universe before the war, it was the biggest source of pride for the entire nation. No one had ever watched the pageant before. The next day, after the great honor bestowed upon us, the whole country watched a tape delay of the Miss Universe pageant. Women wept with Georgina when the announcer said, "Miss Lebanon, you are the new Miss Universe," even though they knew it was coming. Philippe Duke became the man.

The bar was stifling. He saw, at the far end of the room, a boy reveal the breast of a girl and kiss it. She laughed and pushed him away. A couple were necking at the table next to that. Jamal kept pushing his way forward. He followed. Someone pinched his butt. He turned around and saw a handsome man smiling at him. "Hello," the man said. Samir pulled Jamal towards him and told him he was leaving. The cigarette smoke was too much for him.

He was not yet ready for his two worlds to meet.

———

FROM: JOSEPH83@PRODIGY.COM (MR JOSEPH TANYOS)
DATE: FRI, 2 AUG 1996 22:34:18, -0500
SUBJECT: PARLIAMENTARY ELECTIONS

Lebanese Parliamentary Elections

Next week, the Lebanese government will hold its second Parliamentary elections since the "adoption" of the Taif Accord. The requirements of that accord have been waived by the current election law, which is undergoing a court challenge in Lebanon. Election was to be by *Mohafazat* with electors in each of the 6 electoral districts electing their delegates to the 128-seat Parliament. The districts are: North Lebanon, Mount Lebanon, Beirut, Beka'a, Sidon, and Nabatyiah.

This scheme, however, left Walid Jumblatt vulnerable in Mount Lebanon and unable to elect his party members since Mount Lebanon is overwhelmingly Christian and confessional voting is expected. It also left Nabih Berri vulnerable in the South since he lacks support in Tyre and other *cazas* of the Nabatyeh *Mohafazat*. Therefore, in order to insure that pro-Syrian Amal Party candidates can succeed, the two southern districts were combined, adding to Berri's voting strength. In Mount Lebanon, the election will be by *caza*, with the predominant Druze districts voting separately from the rest of Mount Lebanon, so as to assure pro-Syrian Jumblatt victories.

This is a tailor-made election. It seems highly improbable that the political forces in opposition to Syrian hegemony over Lebanon will have an opportunity to elect a significant voting bloc, regardless of the degree of participation by those Lebanese citizens who support such candidates. Due to the Sunni-Frangieh pro-Syrian alliance in the North, North Lebanon will elect pro-Syrian deputies. Due to Hizballah power in the Beka'a, Amal power in the South and Jumblatti power in the Shouf, all of these districts will likewise send pro-Syrian deputies to Parliament. Only in Beirut and the balance of Mount Lebanon is there an opportunity to send opposition deputies to Parliament; however, due to the lack of independent or international monitoring of the election process and the calculation of the results, Syrian intelligence forces will insure that no such opposition forces are elected in any significant numbers.

The 1992 boycott did work. The current parliament represents the will of only 13 percent of the Lebanese voters. As such, it has been rendered illegitimate and incapable of legislating sweeping change to the Lebanese constitution, though it has done its damage.

A 1996 election in which the Lebanese fully participate in a Syrian-controlled process with a Syrian-scripted outcome will not bear democratic fruit. It can only place a very powerful and dangerous weapon into the hands of the Assad regime. The Lebanese government, including the Parliament, is a tool in Syria's hand under the current occupation. As long as those institutions are exposed as Syrian puppets, they do not carry the legitimacy necessary to be dangerous to Lebanese independence. Significant participation by the Lebanese in a Syrian-controlled election can only be compared to sheep silently and voluntarily going under the butcher's knife. A Syrian-controlled Lebanese Parliament which over 50 percent of the Lebanese participated in electing would bear the cloak of legitimacy that the Syrians need in order to fully utilize the hegemony it won over the Lebanese government in 1990 and complete the process of integrating Lebanon into greater Syria by legislative act of a duly elected Lebanese parliament.

For these reasons, I oppose participation in this election unless the voters in all electoral districts are treated equally and international election monitors participate in the process to insure a free and fair result. If these conditions are met, then sure, there should be full participation as the opportunity will exist for creating a significant opposition bloc to the pro-Syrian forces in Parliament. If these conditions are not met and Syrian control of the election is not challenged, then those Lebanese who think they smell the fragrance of freedom in Lebanon are like birds in gilded cages—they have lost sight of the bars that surround them. I urge all Lebanese who read this note that they not become the unwitting accomplices in the demise of their own independence and freedom by lending these fixed elections the legitimacy that only their participation can provide. Boycott these "elections." Do not give the Syrians the victory they desire. Your refusal to vote is a vote against Syrian domination, occupation, and integration of your country into theirs. Insist, with those of your fellow countrymen who are demanding equal treatment, that guarantees of freedom and fairness be the price of your participation in the process.

J. TANYOS
JOSEPH83@PRODIGY.COM
BIRMINGHAM, ALABAMA, USA

———

If there is one statement I hate more than anything else in the world, it's "They say Beirut used to be the Paris of the Middle East." That is so fucking patronizing. I hate it. It is so fucking condescending. Beirut is probably the greatest city in the world. One of the oldest, if not *the* oldest, with more history in one of its neighborhoods than all the cities of the United States. It really irritates me. Of course, the corollary statement, "I hear Beirut used to be the Switzerland of the Middle East" is just as inane. There is no comparison. Paris is Paris and Beirut is Beirut. The people who say such idiotic statements have never been to Beirut, of course. If it weren't for the war, they probably would never have heard of it. Just like people who say, "Some of my best friends are gay." I hate that. I hate people who say that.

The first time I saw the Israeli planes, I was playing soccer. I was at school in Mishref, a town just above Damour. It was physical education class and we were all on the soccer field. The Yom Kippur war of 1973 had just started. They were exciting times. The war was close, but of course, the Lebanese were not involved. Even though Israel always included Lebanon as a participant in the wars against it, that was never really the case. Lebanon may have fought Israel in spirit, but the reality was such that our army was the butt of every joke. The joke was always that the army Lebanon sent to fight the Israelis in 1948 consisted of two men on a motorcycle. It would have been a scooter, but I am not sure they were invented then. I believe the Lebanese Air Force consisted of six Mirages. When France delivered them, they flew one and it crashed, so they left the other five in storage.

The planes must have been attacking the Palestinian camps. The boys just stood on the field in awe. They were so beautiful. Jamal was staring open-mouthed at the planes. Then the miracle happened. On one pass, the planes flew so low, I thought they were going to land on the field. We were able to read their serial numbers. I wanted so much to be up there. A half hour later, they were gone, but the boys were all buzzed.

As time went on, the planes lost their luster. When they started the bombing campaign, which continued throughout the civil war, they became ordinary. When they flew overhead, their sonic booms intending to shatter the Beirutis' nerves, they became a nuisance. Another dream died.

Let us pray.
Lord God,
Almighty Father,
our faith testifies that Your Son
died for us and rose to life again.
May our brother Kurt share in this mystery:
as he has gone to his rest believing in Jesus,
may he come through Him to the joy of resurrection.
We ask you this through Christ our Lord.

Amen.

Lord God,
You are the glory of believers
and the life of the just.
Your son redeemed us
by dying and rising to life again.
Since our brother Kurt believed in the mystery
of our own resurrection,
let him share the joys and blessings
of the life to come.
We ask this through Christ our Lord.

Amen.

FIRST READING
A reading from the book of Wisdom

The souls of the just are in the hand of God,
and no torment shall touch them.
They seemed, in the view of the foolish, to be dead;
and their passing away was through an affliction
and their going forth from us, utter destruction.

But they are in peace.

For if before men, indeed, they be punished,

yet is the hope full of immortality;

Chastised a little, they shall be greatly blessed,

because God tried them

and found them worthy of Himself.

As gold in the furnace, He proved them,

and as sacrificial offerings He took them to Himself.

In the time of their visitation they shall shine,

and shall dart about as sparks through stubble;

They shall judge nations and rule over peoples,

and the Lord shall be their King forever.

Those who trust in Him shall understand truth,

and the faithful shall abide with Him in love:

Because grace and mercy are with His holy ones,

and His care is with His elect.

This is the Word of the Lord.

Thanks be to God.

SECOND READING

A reading from the letter of Paul to the Romans

Are you not aware that we who were baptized into Christ Jesus were baptized into His death? Through baptism into His death we were buried with Him, so that, just as Christ was raised from the dead by the glory of the Father, we too might live a new life.

If we have been united with Him through the likeness to His death, so shall we be through a like resurrection. This we know: our old self was crucified with Him so that the sinful body might be destroyed and we might be slaves to sin no longer. A man who is dead has been freed from sin. If we have died with Christ, we believe that we are also to live with Him. We know that Christ, once raised from the dead, will never die again; death has no more power over Him.

This is the Word of the Lord.

Thanks be to God.

A reading from the holy gospel according to Matthew

Come you whom my Father has blessed.

Jesus said to his disciples: "When the Son of Man comes in His glory, escorted by the angels of heaven, He will sit upon His royal throne, and all the nations will be assembled before Him. Then He will separate them into two groups, as a shepherd separated sheep from goats. The sheep He will place on His right hand, the goats on His left. The King will say to those on his right: 'Come. You have my Father's blessing! Inherit the Kingdom prepared for you from the creation of the world. For I was hungry and you gave me food, I was thirsty and you gave me drink. I was a stranger and you welcomed me, naked and you clothed me. I was ill and you comforted me, in prison and you came to visit me.'

"Then the just will ask him: 'Lord, when did we see you hungry and feed you or see you thirsty and give you drink? When did we welcome you away from home or clothe you in your nakedness? When did we visit you when you were ill or in prison?'

"The King will answer them: 'I assure you, as often as you did it for one of my least brothers, you did it for me.'

"Then He will say to those on His left: 'Out of my sight, you condemned, into the everlasting fire prepared for the devil and his angels! I was hungry and you gave me no food, I was thirsty and you gave me no drink. I was away from home and you gave me no welcome, naked and you gave me no clothing. I was ill and in prison and you did not come to comfort me.'

"They in turn will ask: 'Lord, when did we see you hungry or thirsty or away from home or naked or ill or in prison and not attend you in your needs?'

"He will answer them: 'I assure you, as often as you neglected to do it to one of these least ones, you neglected to do it me.'

"These will go off to eternal punishment and the just to eternal life."

This is the gospel of the Lord.

———

Even as a child, I preferred goat's milk.

———

Deceit is the national pastime. I always felt no Lebanese ever told the truth willingly. An untrained observer might wonder if any business is ever conducted in Lebanon. Westerners are shocked when goods are not delivered, appointments not kept, and promises forgotten.

Appearances being all that matter, truth plays a minor role. Everyone takes part in the illusions, a collective *fata morgana*.

I met him on the way to Beirut. The Middle East Airlines flight was delayed at Heathrow. All the Lebanese passengers took over a lounge at the airport. Everyone seemed to know everyone else, except for me. He was sitting among friends, chatting. I noticed him, for he was handsome.

"How long has it been since you have been back?" I asked him when we were alone.
"It's been about three years," he replied. "How about you?"
"About the same."

I liked him. I assumed he was gay. He gave off all the signals.

"You know, you should take out your earring before you get to the airport." I told him. "I never wear mine in Lebanon."
"Why?" he asked me, shocked.
"Because people will look at you funny. It's not worth the hassle."
"I am not going to," he insisted. "It's part of who I am. I don't see why I have to hide it."

He told me his name was Toufic Ashkar. He was an ER doctor in Detroit. I was impressed. He was only a year older than I was. His family lived in East Beirut. He was there to visit. It was tough getting the time off work, but he managed to get a month's vacation.

"I don't understand why anyone would care if I wore an earring," he went on. "It's my business. Everybody involves themselves in each other's business. I have my life and I intend to live it my way."

I told him I was gay. He said he wasn't. I told him I was HIV-positive. That took him by surprise. He was the first Lebanese I came out to. I was practicing. My mother was next. He was gentle and understanding. His friends called him and he went back to join them. I had given him my phone number in DC. He said he would call me when he got back to Detroit. I welcomed it. I needed a Lebanese friend, someone who would know me as I was. I had separated myself for too long.

When the flight took off, I sat next to a loquacious man. My reading a long novel did not help. He kept chatting endlessly. When he mentioned Toufic Ashkar, my ears perked up. My seatmate was from Detroit as well. He told me Toufic had just been fired from his job as an assistant X-ray technician at Detroit General. His uncle was an administrator at the hospital. He kept transferring his nephew to different departments, hoping he would be competent at something.

When I stood in line to get my passport stamped, he was in the adjacent one. He was not wearing his earring. He never looked my way.

I did not have the courage to come out to my mother. I spared her for two more years.

———

April 11th, 1996
Dear Diary,

For the last couple of days, it seems like the war has never stopped. The Israelis have been bombing Lebanon again. I am so upset. Israeli helicopters conducted a series of air raids over Beirut. They say they want to rout out Hizballah members from their headquarters in the Dahieh. Israel says the goal of the raids was to destroy the Hizballah. Don't they know the only way to destroy Hizballah is for them to leave Lebanon? They say they can't leave until Hizballah stops launching attacks on them. Hizballah won't stop until they leave. Syria collected all the arms from the militias except for Hizballah, which they are using as a pawn to keep the pressure on the Israelis. Yet Israel does not attack the Syrians. The Lebanese eat shit and die.

Hizballah, today, called on their suicide bombers to retaliate. The call for vengeance came after Israel bombed an ambulance, killing six civilians. Images of the dead, a mother with a dead baby on her breast, a child with no face sitting on her father's lap, were broadcast on television yesterday. After all this time, these pictures still horrify me.

You know, Shimon Peres has ordered the attacks to counteract his image of being soft on terrorism before their upcoming elections. We pay with our lives so the bastard can win an election. We pay with our lives so the other bastard, Assad, can get back the Golan Heights. The Americans allow this because they want to save the peace process by making sure Peres gets reelected. Is that ridiculous or what?

How long can this go on? How many more ambulances?

———

I am in Beirut, in a large hall. I notice there are lots of Americans. They must be coming back to the city. It is weird. They all look like they are wearing clothes from the sixties. Maybe the fifties. The double doors open up. Hordes of Americans pour in. These are all men, wearing blue suits from that decade. They all look exactly alike. They must be clones. They probably work for IBM.

———

He told me to kill him. He had said if it ever got rough, he didn't want to go on. If at any time, he couldn't think clearly, or read his books, I was to put an end to his life.

I argued. I begged. To no avail.

His heart rate doubled. They did not know what was going on. The arteries had expanded to three times their normal size. They could not find another case like it. Another new opportunistic infection.

Sleep was almost impossible. He would sit in front of the TV watching talk shows.

I killed him.

———

Since the beginning of the war, a cabdriver by the name of Haj Omar had shuttled people between various places while the war was going on. He risked his life to ensure that essential services remained running in his city. On May 23, 1985, Haj Omar was killed while driving nurses from the American University Hospital to their homes on the East side. In tribute, the doctors, nurses, and orderlies of the hospital, wearing their white coats, walked silently with his relatives and friends in the funeral procession through the streets of Beirut. May he rest in peace.

———

In 1992, I received a call from Jana saying a man had bought the three paintings they had at the gallery. He had asked her if she could procure more paintings. He was interested in paintings from different periods. He was Lebanese. He was shipping the paintings to Beirut.

I did not want to deal directly with him. I would send her some new paintings. She could ask her customers if anybody was willing to sell.

Jana called the following day, insisting they were flying out the next day. The man wanted to visit my studio. I told her Maria would show them around. I was leaving. She did her usual you-may-not-realize-that-this-is-a-business-but-I-have-to-pay-the-rent-and-pay-the-employees-and-what-have-I-done-to-deserve-this routine. I agreed to stay because I lacked the stamina to listen to the routine in its entirety.

They arrived at my studio straight from the airport. He was very businesslike. He was probably already boinking Jana. She was chipper. He bought all three paintings that were out. He asked to see my collection. I told him it was not for sale. He told me which paintings he had already bought. Jana had been busy. He now had one of the best collections of my work. I told him he was not to have any more. I did not want my paintings to end up in Beirut. It was unsafe.

He then did what few people have been able to do. He shocked me. He asked me where I wanted to be buried. The question dumbfounded me. I choked. He said they would be honored if I were buried in Beirut.

I allowed him to buy three paintings from my collection. But only three.

———

The weariest and most loathèd worldly life,
That age, ache, penury, and imprisonment

Can lay on nature is a paradise,
To what we fear of death.

The bard said that. Borges said that in Tlön all men who repeat
one line of Shakespeare *are* William Shakespeare.

———

I am in a gas station filling my white car. The station is spotlessly
clean, unsullied. White neon lights illuminate the night. Everything is white and silver. I have been filling my tank for a long
time and the pump is still going. I look under my car and realize
the gas is going directly to an underground tank in the station.
There is no way I would be able to fill up my car.

———

I am beyond embarrassment at this point. I have seen it all. I
have been through it all.

Nawal wipes my butt. I must have had an accident. She talks to
me constantly. I hear her. I can't seem to think straight. She talks
to me of home. I am home. My mind wanders.

Our roles reverse.

———

In July of 1980, Bashir Gemayel, leader of the Phalange Militia,
united all the Christian militias by force. They were some of the
bloodiest battles of the war. He assassinated many of his rivals.
Stalin would have been proud. He named his new coalition the
Lebanese Forces. Two years later, with the help of the invading Israeli army, he was elected president of Lebanon.

The election of a known murderer to the presidency is not uncommon. Suleiman Franjieh, the man who was president when the war started, was known to have killed twelve people of a rival Christian clan while they were praying in church. Coitus interruptus.

Bashir Gemayel was elected on August 23, 1982. He lasted until September 14, when he was assassinated by the Syrians. The Israelis moved into West Beirut, which they had promised they would not do, to protect the population. Hundreds of Palestinian civilians were massacred in Sabra and Chatilla by members of the Lebanese Forces, who were able to enter West Beirut with the Israelis. All of which led Menachem Begin to say, "Goyim kill goyim, and they always blame us," or something to that effect.

The leader of the militiamen who committed the atrocities was an Israeli-trained killer by the name of Elie Hobeika. Later on during the war, when the Lebanese Forces went through another internal cleanup, Hobeika fled and took asylum in Syria, once his sworn enemy. When Syria won the war, which they were allowed to by the Americans because of their help in the new world order against Saddam Hussein, Hobeika became a minister in the government of Lebanon.

He still is today. I believe he is the minister of tourism, as well as a presidential candidate.

Lest you think that Bashir Gemayel's stay in the presidency was the shortest one, I have to tell you the story of René Mouawad. Poor René. He was elected president; this time, instead of with Israeli help, it was with Syrian help, in November of 1989. He did not make the end of the month. He was assassinated on November 22.

Embassies had to constantly change pictures.

———

Mark Lietbarsky
920 29th Street NW
Washington, DC 20007

Dear Mark,

Thank you so much for your kind letter. I am sorry I was unable to get back to you earlier. As you can imagine, events have been somewhat overwhelming. The funeral took a lot out of us. It was gratifying to note how much my mother was loved. It is only now, forty days later, that I have some time for myself. There has been a continuous flow of people coming to pay their respects.

The funeral was very tough on us. I wish you could have been able to be here. She loved you so much. I am so sorry you are not doing so well. Your health was always on my mother's mind.

Listen, Mark. As soon as I have affairs taken care of on this end, I intend to come see you for a long visit. That should be in three weeks or so. I understand you have everything under control and your family is taking care of you. I will come over to help in any way I can. My mother would have wanted that and I want to. Please, there is no point in trying to dissuade me. My mind is already made up.

As for my mother's diaries, I am afraid it is highly unlikely they will ever be published. I have read them, so has my father. You are

214

right. They are incredibly moving. I went through the entire gamut of emotions reading them. Everything you said in your letter was true. We would be doing "the world" a favor by publishing them. However, what may be difficult for you to grasp is the kind of society we live in. Most of us prefer not to see. It is as simple as that. Publishing the diaries would create a world of problems. We can start with the family, the immediate and the extended. My sisters think their life would become a living hell if anyone even suspected the diaries exist. They consider laying bare our mother's life to be nothing short of criminal. What they are saying in reality is they would feel shamed. Even if my mother's diaries did not include the personal materials they do, revealing them would be a scandal. We simply do not understand Western culture's fascination with biographies, or worse, the current obsession with telling it all to Oprah and her ilk. A person's life is kept very private in our culture. Although we tend to be emotional people, we do not reveal personal feelings or share them. Any kind of personal revelation is treated with disdain. Lebanese society would ostracize the perpetrator and their family.

It is not simply that my mother wrote openly about Samir's sexuality and AIDS that we feel the way we do about this, although it is a major concern. Even though I am sure everyone in Lebanon knows Samir died of AIDS, no one openly talks about it. The family prefers the subject never be discussed. Even if AIDS was never mentioned in her diaries, the mere fact she wrote down her honest feelings about her life and the people who are a part of it, would force our society to look at issues it considers best left unmentioned. The ostrich prefers to keep her head buried. Light is too painful. Please, do not judge us too harshly. It is just the way we are.

There are also other issues which make the diaries problematic. My mother wrote about politics and politicians. For the first time in Lebanon, we are living under a regime where it is no longer acceptable to openly and honestly criticize our government's policies. Men and women have disappeared for mentioning much less than what my mother wrote about Assad. All the war criminals are now "respected" politicians. It is getting better where we are now able to criticize our government somewhat, but my mother actually wrote the truth about the leader of our "beloved" neighbor. The whole family could end up in the *Mazzeh,* the infamous Syrian prison.

It would take an incredible amount of courage to publish these diaries, something neither I, nor anyone in my family, possesses. I am a coward. I hope you understand. I know this will disappoint you because it means so much to you. I do apologize.

I will call you soon to tell you about my plans. Hopefully, by the time I get there, you will be feeling better. In the meantime, take good care of yourself and God bless you.

Sincerely,

Your good friend,
Joumana

SUBJECT: REASONS TO GET THE SYRIANS OUT OF
LEBANON
FROM: JHNOUB@AOL.COM
DATA: TUE, 26 MAR 1996 02:15:56 -0500

The government is Syrian, not Lebanese. Every minister was appointed by Syria and anyone who does not toe the line is forced to resign.
The president is a Syrian puppet. He was forced on us by Syria.

He does nothing without Syria's okay. He is nothing but a Syrian dog.

We have no free elections. What is the point of voting if they keep rigging up the election to make sure their politicians win?

We have pictures of Assad all over Lebanon. It is as if he were our president. When his son died, Beirut was forced to close down for three days of mourning.

Our economy exists only to serve Syria. The national bank cannot make a move without Syria's approval.

Our army does only what Syria wants. They beat up on their own people, but leave Hizballah alone because Syria wants them to.

We are the nuclear dump of the world. Syrians take money and allow Italian ships to dump their nuclear wastes on Lebanese soil.

We have no human rights. People are being kidnapped and tortured constantly. Amnesty International has a huge list of human rights abuses in Lebanon.

No project can be built in Beirut without bribing Syrian officials. The current rate is twenty percent off the top. No boulevard, no bridge, no power plant, nothing can be built without the Syrians getting paid.

The hashish and opium trade is now completely in Syrian hands. They are making their money forcing our farmers in the Beka'a valley to plant nothing but drugs.

There are over one million Syrian workers in Lebanon. They are destroying our economy and taking food off our tables.

Criminals roam the streets. Jail is used only for government opponents.

Our children are being forced to study according to Syrian standards. They are being brainwashed into accepting Syrian rule.

The Lebanese are second-class citizens in our own country.

Shops in Beirut have to pay Syrians to remain open.

Our lands are being sold to Arabs and rich Syrians. No Lebanese family can afford an apartment in Beirut anymore.

Beirut is the headquarters of international terrorism again.

Our foreign policy is Syrian foreign policy. We cannot deal with any other country directly. We have to wait and see what Syria will allow us to do.

The guns have not been silenced. They have simply begun using silencers when killing.

Our people are dying.

In simple terms, we have been sacrificed to the peace process and the new world order.

FROM: SAID MALEH

SUBJECT: TO THOSE LEBANESE WHO CANNOT DEAL WITH THE TRUTH

I have been sitting here listening to all you people talk about the Israeli occupation of South Lebanon. You people have no idea what you are talking about. You live in nice houses in France, Canada, and America and think you know what is going on. Did any one of you think of asking those of us who live in the South what we think? No, you did not think of asking. Well, guess what? I am going to tell you anyway.

First of all, I only want to talk to the Lebanese living abroad. I do not care to talk to those who live under Syrian occupation. The latter group has been brainwashed for so long it is completely hopeless to try and reason with them. Only after the last trace of the Syrian evil has been erased from our country can we hope to have a reasonable debate. Until then, we will just bide our time until all of Lebanon is liberated. The time for debating with the Syrians and their proxies is over.

History will be the final arbiter of truth. I have watched the discussions of liberating the South, not knowing how you people could think of Israel as the occupier. Israel is the liberator of South Lebanon. The Israelis are here to protect us against the terror that is Hizballah. If you consider Israel as the occupier, then you have to say that America was the occupier of Great Britain during World War II. Have you thought about that? Hizballah train their men to kill women and children of the South. They are killing the people of the South, destroying our homes and businesses, raping our lands. Yet you people think of Hizballah as the defenders of the South. Israel is not an occupier of South Lebanon. Why don't you people, who think you know everything, come down to the South and see for yourselves? Come down and ask the people who they are afraid of, the Israelis or Hizballah. Stop living in your ivory towers and reading all the false propaganda being distributed by the Syrian regime and their sycophants. Come see how our Lebanese families struggle under the Hizballah oppression. After you see all that, then maybe you can decide which is the free Lebanon.

I have heard you people talk of Lebanon under the Hariri government as the free Lebanon and the South as the occupied Lebanon. History will prove that you are wrong. When Chiang Kai-shek ruled over Taiwan, everybody thought he was an evil dictator, whereas now he is considered a hero. They considered mainland China the good China and Taiwan the bad China. You cannot make a fool of history. Everybody now knows that Taiwan is the good China. The same thing will happen with Saad Haddad. Like Chiang Kai-shek, he is the true liberator of Lebanon. Just because world opinion has a distorted view of the situation does not make it true. Just like Taiwan, South Lebanon will soon be recognized as the good Lebanon and Lebanon under the Hariri government as the bad Lebanon. In the end, the truth always comes out.

The truth will finally show us that the Israelis are liberating us from the heavy Syrian boots and protecting us from the Hizballah

Nazis. Just you wait and see. All of you will regret everything you are saying right now. When the truth finally comes out, you will all pretend that you knew all along which was the free Lebanon, just like everybody pretends now that they knew all along that Taiwan was really the free China. You will all hail Saad Haddad as the true hero that he is.

The South will be vindicated. The lies you are spreading, knowingly or unknowingly, will be shown for what they are. In time, you will all come to see who was right. The South will lead the way to a completely free Lebanon.

Long live South Lebanon and long live our Israeli friends.

Sincerely,

Said Maleh
Jezzine, Free South Lebanon

FROM: IDABOU@AOL.COM
DATA: TUE, 19 MAR 1996 20:21:47 -0500
SUBJECT: RESPONSE TO PIERRE MBAYED

Where do you come off, Mr. Mbayed? How could you decipher what I said that way? I said, "Many of my friends are Christians and I love them very much." How could you even think that what I meant was that most Christians are horrible people, but some of my Christian friends are not too bad . . . Huh? I cannot fathom how you would even say such a thing. Can't you read? No, Pierre, I do not hate Christians and I am not an isolationist. Fuck you.

I am getting a major headache.

The first time my mother met Mark she did not like him. I did not expect her to. It was difficult enough for her dealing with my sexuality and health. She was in no mood to like my lover. I am sure she also deduced he was the one who unknowingly infected me with the virus.

Every time I called Beirut to talk to her, I would make sure to mention something nice about Mark. It wasn't difficult because he treated me so well. We had been together for nine years. She always changed the subject. It became a contest of wills between us. For a long time, she won.

It was not until her visit two months ago that she saw in him what I saw. She was shocked as to how weak I had gotten. She saw for the first time how much he loved me. I saw her writing furiously in her diary. When she finished, it was obvious she had made a decision.

She adopted Mark.

Sometimes, I thought about writing a play. It would be easier than writing a whole book. I would be able to put down the whole complex idea of Lebanese life as a conversation between two upper-class Lebanese women. It might go something like this:

The play takes place in a restaurant café in Paris, Les Deux Magots in St. Germain. The set must have an awning with the name of the restaurant. It is the place to be seen in for the Lebanese. The play has two major characters, and a minor one, the waiter who serves them. He has an attitude, of course. Sylvie is a Christian Lebanese woman residing in Paris. Amal is a Muslim Lebanese who visits Paris often. Both are dressed in designer suits, impeccably accessorized. They have the same blond dye job, the same coif, and both are thin. They look like clones with matching oufits.

Sylvie enters the stage. She sees Amal sitting at the table. Amal stands up to greet her. At the table, they kiss three times. The kisses are air kisses. Touching cheek to cheek and kissing air. Beginning on the left cheek, right cheek, and back to the left. They sit. The waiter hovers.

AMAL: *(to the waiter)* Deux cafés.

The waiter leaves.

SYLVIE: Sorry I'm late but I could not find a taxi. Have you been waiting long?

AMAL: Oh no. I just got here myself.

SYLVIE: Did you have a good flight?

AMAL: It was hell. The service on MEA is awful. I'm taking Air France from now on.

SYLVIE: Good for you. I always do. It's the only way.

AMAL: So when are you coming down?

SYLVIE:	The thirteenth. I haven't been down in four months.
AMAL:	I know. So how is everybody?
SYLVIE:	Everybody is doing well. Jean works so hard I hardly see him. Did I tell you about Patrick?
AMAL:	No. How is he?
SYLVIE:	He graduated the top of his class at the London Polytechnic. He has been accepted into a business program run by Harvard in conjunction with the Sorbonne.

(The waiter brings the coffee. They completely ignore him.)

AMAL:	That's wonderful. Is he going to move back here or live in Boston?
SYLVIE:	It's here in Paris. It's wonderful. I am sure he will have to fly to Boston every now and then.
AMAL:	I am so happy for you. If he does fly to Boston, tell him to look up Murwan.
SYLVIE:	Is he still at MIT?
AMAL:	Yes. He should be done with his master's in a couple of years.
SYLVIE:	You must be so proud of him.

AMAL: I am. I am, darling. He is just so bright.

SYLVIE: So what is the latest?

AMAL: Not much. Things have been slow in Beirut.

SYLVIE: That is not always a bad thing.

AMAL: I know. Did you hear that Marie-Christine's eldest son got married?

SYLVIE: Yes, of course. How was the wedding? I heard they spent a fortune.

AMAL: They sure did. Would you believe three million dollars?

SYLVIE: You have to be kidding.

AMAL: No. I swear.

SYLVIE: Are they that rich?

AMAL: My dear, where have you been? The Ballans are loaded. From Africa. Their main business is in Liberia. Pharmaceuticals, car dealerships, gas stations, rubber plants, you name it. They are very rich. They practically run that country. They were the first Lebanese there.

SYLVIE: I bet it was awful.

AMAL: *Awful* does not begin to describe it. A complete disaster. You should have seen the dress. It cost half a million dollars and it was the ugliest thing.

SYLVIE: Half a million? My God, who designed it?

AMAL: You're not going to believe it. *(Pause.)* Some American designer.

SYLVIE: American?

(Amal nods her head. They are looking at each other, when they both start laughing. Not too loudly. It lasts for at least a minute. Sylvie tries to stop laughing. She places her hand on Amal's hand, hoping to control herself. They stop for a second. Then they have another fit of giggling.)

SYLVIE: Why? My God, why would they do that?

AMAL: They wanted something different, they said. For that kind of money, they could have had a Montana.

SYLVIE: A Léger.

AMAL: A Versace.

SYLVIE: That poor girl.

AMAL: No, my dear. Poor Marie-Christine. Just imagine what she had to go through at that wedding.

225

SYLVIE: Oh, the poor dear.

AMAL: The Ballan girl is incredibly ugly. I can't
                  imagine what her son saw in her.

SYLVIE: As ugly as the Bandoura girl?

AMAL: No, my dear, that one is really ugly. This one
                  is close, though.

SYLVIE: That one was so ugly. I couldn't believe she
                  found a husband.

AMAL: Money, dear, money. Daddy has money.

SYLVIE: All I have to say is Patrick better not bring
                  me some ugly girl. I would have none of it.

AMAL: Is he seeing anybody?

SYLVIE: Not right now. He was seeing an English girl
                  for a while. I put a stop to that.

AMAL: Good for you. You don't want people to talk
                  too much.

SYLVIE: I'll find him a suitable girl when the time
                  comes.

AMAL: So how is Manal?

SYLVIE: She gained all the weight she lost.

AMAL: I thought she was on a strict diet.

SYLVIE: Not anymore.

(Sylvie opens her purse and offers Amal a cigarette, and takes one herself. Amal uses her designer lighter to light both of them.)

SYLVIE: What else is going on?

AMAL: Not much. Amin Dabyan is getting married.

SYLVIE: He's such a handsome boy. Who's the fool?

AMAL: The same girl he's been going out with for years.

SYLVIE: The Makarem girl? I would think her father would not approve.

AMAL: Oh, he doesn't. There is not much he can do. She's a headstrong girl.

SYLVIE: But she was married once before.

AMAL: Yes. It lasted six months.

SYLVIE: And her father still lets her do what she wants?

AMAL: They both are heavy cocaine users, so her father just doesn't know what to do.

SYLVIE: She was always trouble. She was in Janine's
                 class. She was trouble then.

AMAL: Well, here's a tidbit that will amuse you, dear.
                 They are saying her first marriage was not
                 consummated.

SYLVIE: What?

AMAL: That's what the Dabyans are saying. Her first
                 marriage was not consummated. She is still a
                 virgin.

SYLVIE: What?

*(Repeat the first laughing scene. Amal nods her head. They look at
each other and start laughing. It goes on for a while as they try to
compose themselves.)*

SYLVIE: She's still a virgin?

AMAL: That's what they say.

SYLVIE: And the abortion she had before she got mar-
                 ried the first time?

AMAL: It never happened.

SYLVIE: Will miracles never cease?

*(More laughter. Amal takes out some tissues from her purse and
gives one to Sylvie. They both wipe tears from their eyes delicately.)*

SYLVIE:	I guess her first child will proclaim himself to be the Lord, as well.
AMAL:	No chance. After the abortion, something went wrong. She can't have any more children.
SYLVIE:	I didn't know that. Why would the boy want to marry her then?
AMAL:	Must be the money or the drugs. They have been doing the nasty for a couple of years.
SYLVIE:	Yes, but she remains a virgin.
AMAL:	Absolutely.
SYLVIE:	You know that slut, and I do use the description judiciously, was not a virgin when she was in Janine's class. She must have been fourteen or fifteen, and was sleeping around then.
AMAL:	Speaking of sluts, you know the youngest Takla girl, Samira?
SYLVIE:	Who is she sleeping with now?
AMAL:	I don't know his name, but he is seventeen.
SYLVIE:	Oh, my God. How old is she? Twenty-four?
AMAL:	Something like that.

SYLVIE: Tragic. Tragic. Anyway, I have some news. Do
             you know Fadia's boy?

AMAL: The homosexual?

SYLVIE: You knew he was homosexual?

AMAL: Of course, dear. Well, suspected really. How
             old is he? Thirty? A bachelor living in Cali-
             fornia?

SYLVIE: That's true. But I never wanted to say any-
             thing. Too embarrassing for Fadia. Anyway,
             he has AIDS.

AMAL: No?

SYLVIE: It's true. It's gotten to the point where he
             couldn't hide it anymore.

AMAL: Poor Fadia. What is she going to do?

SYLVIE: She's telling everybody he has leukemia.

AMAL: The poor thing. She's probably going through
             hell. Everybody will start talking behind her
             back.

SYLVIE: I felt so sorry for her. I saw her last week. She
             pretended everything was okay, but you could
             tell.

AMAL: Poor Fadia.

230

SYLVIE:	This topic is too distressing. What do you want to do? Do you want to go to the Faubourg and see what they have?
AMAL:	Yes, that sounds lovely. Where's our waiter?
SYLVIE:	Probably resting. These French work so hard.

(Both giggle.)

SYLVIE:	You're coming with us to dinner, right?
AMAL:	No, I can't.
SYLVIE:	You must. I won't have it. You must come.
AMAL:	Are you sure?
SYLVIE:	I must insist.
AMAL:	Okay. I'll break my diet for tonight only.
SYLVIE:	Good girl. Now, where's that damn waiter?

I never wrote that play. I did not know how. I sat for days, trying to figure how to put words on paper, but to no avail.

———

The music comes back again. Voluptuous. The violins sing. A siren's song. The dark is all enveloping. The time is near.

———

March 19th, 1996
Dear Diary,

I am unable to stop feeling guilty. Mark tells me it is normal.
Bless him, he has been so helpful. I still am unable to stop these
bad feelings. I feel I have been a bad mother.

What mother would wish her son dead? I wished Samir dead. I
kept hoping it would be all over. I tried to suppress those feelings
during his last month. They kept popping up. I could not control
them.

I sometimes rationalize it by saying he was dying anyway. There
was no hope. He was suffering and I prayed for his death to end
his suffering. In reality, I wished for his death to end my suffering. I wanted to come back to Beirut. I hate to admit it, and I pray
for God's forgiveness, but he became an inconvenience. I wished
it was over.

Mark says that is quite common. Even he felt that at times. But
he was my son. I loved him so much. I know Mark loved him, but
it is not the same thing. I just pray Samir never realized what I
was thinking at the end.

I am weak. I have always been weak. What can I say? I hope he
can forgive me.

———

The city was not completely divided yet when my cousin Neyla
drove back from her job in a bank on the East side to her house
on the West. There was heavy traffic. They must have installed a
new checkpoint.

As her car got closer to the bottleneck, she saw the militiamen. She was terrified. As she got even closer, she realized this would be her last day. It was a scene from the Apocalypse. The militiamen would look at the ID card. They would then either let the car pass or ask it to park at the side. When the car was parked, more armed men would ask the passengers to get out of the car. They would ask them to move next to a dead pile. They would then shoot them, adding to the dead pile, men, women, and children. A couple of militiamen would then drive the cars to a parking lot, clearing space for new cars. But the pile kept growing. The victims followed orders.

The fear you experience when you are about to face a violent death is indescribable. You shake, uncontrollably. You sweat, profusely. You lose control of motor coordination. Your bowels fail you. You either are unable to speak or blabber continuously.

Neyla was the next car coming up. The car in front of her passed. It was her turn. The militiaman asked for her ID when she heard a young man's voice say, "Let her pass. She used to be my neighbor." Georges smiled at her and waved her through. She was weeping uncontrollably when she heard Georges tell another boy, "Her sister was the best fuck."

———

"Let there be light!" said God, and there was light!
"Let there be blood!" says man, and there's a sea!

Hail Lord Byron, an honest bisexual.

———

233

When the Israelis entered the mountains, they encountered the least resistance. It was not because the Druze were not fierce fighters. The Israelis simply sent in their own Druze contingents first. There were a few Druze battalions in the Israeli army. The part of Lebanon which had rarely been conquered through the ages was like a cakewalk for the invading Israeli Army. The two staunch defenders of the mountains, the Maronites and the Druze, were not fighting. The Maronites were the Israeli allies and the Druze could not fire on relatives from across the border.

Mrs. Talhouk lived in a house, on the edge of Ain Unoub, a small Druze town. Her house had miraculously escaped any damage throughout the war. When the Israelis were outside her village, they sent warning that they were going to bomb, because they knew *terrorists* were hiding in the village. They advised the villagers if their house had no *terrorists,* they should raise a visible white flag on top of the house. They would try not to shell white-flagged houses. Mrs. Talhouk took out all her white bed sheets and towels, and hung them on the laundry lines on her roof. Every fifteen minutes she would run up to the roof, like a hysterical woman, and shake the sheets, hoping they would be seen by the Israelis. It became an obsession.

Mrs. Talhouk's house survived the Israeli invasion. It did not survive *New Jersey.* When the Israelis withdrew, the massacres between the Druze and Maronites, which became known as the War of the Mountain, began. The Druze seemed to be winning, when the Americans got involved in the war, openly. They used the *New Jersey* battleship's sixteen-inch guns to bomb Druze villages. All it took was one sixteen-inch shell to destroy her home. It was a two-hundred-year-old house.

America entered the Lebanese Civil War. It paid the price. Two hundred marines were killed by one Shiite. Reagan pulled the troops and avoided discussing Lebanon. Lebanon, like AIDS, was hardly ever mentioned by our president.

―――――

Borges said things lost their detail when people forgot them. A stone threshold lasted as long as it was visited by a beggar, and faded from sight on his death. Occasionally, a few birds have saved the ruins of an amphitheater.

Calvino said a book does not exist if it is not read.

Sandra Bernhard said without you, she's nothing.

So kiss my ass, motherfuckers. Yippy kay yay.

―――――

I would like to show you an editorial from the *Jerusalem Post*. It explains the current political situation in Lebanon fairly well.

Lebanon First

Editorial

(August 13, 1996)—Syria's rejection of Prime Minister Binyamin Netanyahu's proposal to resume peace talks based on the concept of "Lebanon first" should lay to rest any illusions in the West about President Hafez Assad's desire for peace with Israel. By rejecting such an eminently reasonable and sensible overture, the Syrian dictator has demonstrated once again that he is in no particular rush to come to terms.

Netanyahu's proposal is that Israel and Syria should resume talks in the U.S. in an effort to build trust and inspire mutual confidence between the two sides. The prime minister stated that Israel would be prepared to withdraw its troops from the security zone in southern Lebanon if three conditions are met: the disarming of Hizballah, the deployment of the Lebanese army to the international border with Israel, and the granting of guarantees concerning the protection of Israel's Christian allies in southern Lebanon.

As the prime minister noted in his address, the situation in Lebanon is truly Kafkaesque. Netanyahu stated, "Here is a situation where the Israeli prime minister announces that he wants to withdraw from the territory of an Arab state—Lebanon. But the Syrian government, together with the Lebanese, are opposing this withdrawal."

Indeed, one cannot help but wonder whether Syria, its rhetoric notwithstanding, is truly interested in an Israeli withdrawal from southern Lebanon. The presence of Israeli forces in Lebanon provides the Assad regime with a rallying cry, and enables Syria to justify the presence of its own occupation army, which controls two-thirds of Lebanese soil.

Were Israel to withdraw, international pressure would almost certainly mount on Syria to pull back its forces as well, something that Assad, who views Lebanon as part and parcel of Greater Syria, is not particularly inclined to do. Leaving Lebanon would also require Syria to give up on the profitable opium and hashish industry that it oversees and cultivates in the Beka'a Valley, which has proven to be an important source of revenue for senior Syrian officials.

Netanyahu's proposal should also help remove doubts about his diplomatic skills. Less than two months into his administration, Netanyahu has shrewdly succeeded in maneuvering the Syrian leader firmly into a corner, forcing the latter to come across as the rejectionist in the eyes of the world. This is no small achievement, given Assad's reputation for being a clever and calculating political operator. By placing the ball squarely in Assad's court, and outfoxing him in the process, Netanyahu has demonstrated not only that he is interested in peace, but that he can also play the game of international diplomacy with the best of them.

Personally, I loved the word *Kafkaesque*. I am not sure the situation in Lebanon is truly Kafkaesque. I don't think Kafka could have possibly thought of a scenario like Lebanon, with the Israelis and Syrians.

I also loved that Netanyahu can play the game of international diplomacy. Now I can sleep better at night.

———

I was sitting, smoking a pipe by the fire, when Updike asked me, "What more fiendish proof of cosmic irresponsibility than a Nature which, having invented sex as a way to mix genes, then permits to arise, amid all its perfumed and hypnotic inducements to mate, a tireless tribe of spirochetes and viruses that torture and kill us for following orders?"

"You said a mouthful, John," I replied. "How else would we become adults?"

John nodded approvingly. We had these conversations often, Updike and I. I provided him with an invaluable service.

I wanted to write a book once. It was to be a biography of Jean Genet as he died of AIDS complications. There were many biographies of him, so I never began the book.

I decided to write a roman à clef. It was to be the story of Ronald Reagan as he grew up in Lebanon. It was more a love story than a biography. Ronald meets Nancy Davis, a third-rate Lebanese actress who has been in a few Egyptian television series. They fall in love. She tells him to kill a few of his rivals while they are praying in church. He does and is elected president of Lebanon during its years of turmoil. I finished the first chapter of the book, but I could not go on because I was unable to find the published research.

I decided to write a meta-fiction book. I would have to write a book that included every quotation from page 244 till page 328 of *The International Thesaurus of Quotations*. The quotations do not have to appear in order. The only requirement is every quotation appears at least once as part of the story. I never started that book since I became more interested in writing a short story as an interview with Oscar Wilde, where he would have to answer all my questions with each of his famous quotes.

I saw a Website which listed the winners of the worst-analogies-ever-written-in-a-high-school-essay contest. I decided to write a novelette that included every one of the analogies listed. They were inspiring. I thought the novelette would be magnificent. I listed the analogies for inspiration:

He spoke with the wisdom that can only come from experience, like a guy who went blind because he looked at a solar eclipse without one of those boxes with a pinhole in it and now goes around the country speaking at high schools about the dangers of looking at a solar eclipse without one of those boxes with a pinhole in it.

She caught your eye like one of those pointy hook latches that used to dangle from screen doors and would fly up whenever you banged the door open again.

The little boat gently drifted across the pond exactly the way a bowling ball wouldn't.

McBride fell twelve stories, hitting the pavement like a Hefty Bag filled with vegetable soup.

From the attic came an unearthly howl. The whole scene had an eerie, surreal quality, like when you're on vacation in another city and *Jeopardy* comes on at 7 P.M. instead of 7:30.

Her hair glistened in the rain like nose hair after a sneeze.

Her eyes were like two brown circles with big black dots in the center.

He was as tall as a six-foot–three-inch tree.

The hailstones leaped from the pavement, just like maggots when you fry them in hot grease.

Her date was pleasant enough, but she knew that if her life was a movie, this guy would be buried in the credits as something like "Second Tall Man."

Long separated by cruel fate, the star-crossed lovers raced across the grassy field toward each other like two freight trains, one having left Cleveland at 6:36 P.M. traveling at 55 mph, the other from Topeka at 4:19 P.M. at a speed of 35 mph.

The politician was gone but unnoticed, like the period after the Dr. on a Dr Pepper can.

They lived in a typical suburban neighborhood with picket fences that resembled Nancy Kerrigan's teeth.

Her vocabulary was as bad as, like, whatever.

John and Mary had never met. They were like two hummingbirds who had also never met.

The thunder was ominous-sounding, much like the sound of a thin sheet of metal being shaken backstage during the storm scene in a play.

His thoughts tumbled in his head, making and breaking alliances like underpants in a dryer without Cling Free.

But my thoughts had no Cling Free, either. I wasn't able to write the novelette.

I adjusted my thinking. I would write a book of short stories. I had collected a series of headlines that have appeared in respectable newspapers. I would write a story with each headline as the title. "Police Begin Campaign to Run Down Jaywalkers" could be an interesting story. That was in the *Los Angeles Times*. I also thought "Lung Cancer in Women Mushrooms" might make a good Calvino. "Astronaut Takes Blame for Gas in Spacecraft" had infinite possibilities.

I never got past "Include Your Children When Baking Cookies."
It was a fun story, but didn't lead anywhere.

I wanted to write a book of strange prose, but life beat me to it.

————

Verdi's *Requiem* overpowers the room. Pavarotti and Ramey are
having a testosterone duel. My dick is bigger than yours. No, my
dick is bigger. Jesus, Jesus, you're number one.

The lights are dim. A cool summer night in San Francisco. A
light breeze flows through the windows. Trumpets blow through
my soul. It's a full moon. Pavarotti wins. Ramey has a deeper
voice, bigger balls. Pavarotti is more confident, bigger dick.

I have a thing for church music. I wonder why. Beethoven's *Missa
Solemnis* is the most beautiful music I have ever heard. Rossini's
Petite Messe Solennelle is divine. My favorite masses are not usu-
ally considered the spiritual ones. Still, they do talk to the divine.
Maybe I yearn for something. The mezzo-soprano sings. Beauti-
ful voice.

The day of wrath, that day
will dissolve the world in ashes,
so say David and Sibyl.

What am I to say, wretch that I am?
Whom shall I ask to intercede for me,
when scarcely the righteous may be secure?

I wonder why. Not for long, though. I get another attack of diar-
rhea and run to the bathroom.

Remember, Merciful Jesus,
I am the cause for Thy journey:
do not abandon me on that day.
Seeking me, Thou didst sit down weary,
Thou didst redeem me, having endured the Cross:
let not such great suffering have been in vain.

Time. What time is it? Butter crumpets and tea. That's what I want. Bring me some butter crumpets and tea, Maria. It's probably late. I don't hear anybody moving. I would settle for scones and clotted cream with my tea. Something English. That's what I want. I am too tired of America and Americans. Still they are better than the French. I hate the French, probably more than I hate Americans. Such arrogant bastards. I once walked into Carvil on Pierre Charron and the salesman took one look at me and said, *"Nous n'avons pas votre pointure, monsieur."* That fucker. A fucking shoe salesman and he's arrogant. I just walked out the door and didn't make a scene for once. We don't have your shoe size. I should have bought the store just to fire him, but that happens only in the movies. I saw *Delta Force,* a terrible movie. The movie is about a hijacking. A group of Arabs hijack a plane and fly it to Beirut. The Delta Force, an American antiterrorist group, comes to Beirut, kills all the bad guys, and saves all the hostages. The hijackers are all unkempt and dirty looking. They look like me on a good day. They are all evil. The Christians and Jews are all wonderful. All the Lebanese, even those not involved in the hijacking, are evil. Anyway, why is it *pointure*? Why not *taille*? Why do the French have a different word for shoe size and clothes size? Because they are arrogant, that's why. Okay, I grant you, they have a right to be arrogant. Any culture that can produce Mallarmé

242

has something to be proud of. But why do shoe salesmen have to be so arrogant? But they are better than the Lebanese. The Lebanese are just arrogant. I fucking hate the Lebanese. I hate them. They are so fucked up. They think they are so great, and for what reason? Has there been a single artist of note? A scientist, an athlete? They are so proud of Gibran. Probably the most overrated writer in history. I don't think any Lebanese has ever read him. If they had, they would keep their mouth fucking shut. At least the French are talented. I was riding the Metro in Paris once and this fourteen-year-old kid came on. He was wearing a black Guns & Roses T-shirt and carrying an accordion. I thought that was such a dichotomy. Fingers proceeded to dance on the instrument. He played *"Sous le Ciel de Paris,"* and I have never heard it played like that. Fingers moved so elegantly. French jazz. He came around collecting money and I gave him a five-hundred-franc note. His eyes got so wide. He looked so cute. I got out at my stop. Would the Lebanese ever produce anybody of that talent? Hardly. Those fuckers are too busy judging everybody else's life to live their own. The happiest day in my life was when I got my American citizenship and was able to tear up my Lebanese passport. That was great. Then I got to hate Americans. And I really do. They are dumb. That's my problem with Americans. They are naïve and dumb. And I hate that. Some movie. Forget the fact some Shiites kidnapped Americans and kept them hostage for years, and Delta Force couldn't do shit. Forget the fact that in one scene they have to cross a cotton field in Beirut. A cotton field in Beirut? At least they do not put a scene in a desert with camels. America is the birthplace of *Wheel of Fortune* and I will never forgive it for that. I'm getting tired. What time is it? I want tea. I want something. The Lebanese would never ride the Paris Metro. The best public transportation in the world. The Lebanese brag that they gave the world the alphabet. I tried so hard to rid myself of anything Lebanese. I hate everything Lebanese. But I never could. It seeps through my entire being. The harder I tried, the more it showed up in the unlikeliest of places. But I never gave up. I do not want to be considered a Lebanese. But that is not up to me. Would people think of me as a painter or a Lebanese painter? That is not up to me.

Nothing in my life is up to me.

One of the hijackers in the movie tells the hostages that the *New Jersey* bombed Lebanon. The priest, one of the hostages, denies it. He says Americans never bombed Beirut. There is no rebuttal. When the hijacked plane lands in Beirut, one of the passengers said this used to be a wonderful city. You could do whatever you want. I couldn't believe what he said next. Beirut used to be the Las Vegas of the Middle East.

Now that's fucking insulting.

———

Death comes in many shapes and sizes, but it always comes. No one escapes the little tag on the big toe.

The four horsemen approach.

The rider on the red horse says, "This good and faithful servant is ready. He knoweth war."

The rider on the black horse says, "This good and faithful servant is ready. He knoweth plague."

The rider on the pale horse says, "This good and faithful servant is ready. He knoweth death."

The rider on the white horse says, "I love you, Mohammad."

The propitious rider on the white horse leads us away.

I die.